CHAINS.

Time to shut up and read.

This muthafuckin book belongs to

Legal Bullshit

Wings of Vitriol icon was created by Khurt Khave using an edited source image created by Rore tattoos-and-doodles.blogspot.com and used under CC BY-SA 3.0 US

The Disneyesque Alice images are derivative works based on the public domain images from the *Alice in Wonderland (1951)* trailer as well as allowed by fair use as parody and social commentary under the Copyright Act of 1976, 17 U.S.C. - 107

Any imagery which may resemble existing images or icons are derivative works created specifically for the purpose of parody and social commentary and are allowed by fair use as parody and social commentary under the Copyright Act of 1976, 17 U.S.C. - 107

The character of Jenny Everywhere is available for use by anyone, with only one condition. This paragraph must be included in any publication involving Jenny Everywhere, in order that others may use this property as they wish. All rights reversed.

The illustration of Jenny Everywhere is by Diana Nock and used under CC BY-SA 3.0 US

Dirty Weasel commission - name withheld at artist's request.

All other images and icons are derivative works of public domain images and/or created wholely by Khurt Khave. All photographs are used with permission from the models (Christine, Isabelle, and Johnna) and photographers (Me and Josh, yo)

Text copyright Khurt Khave

Acknowledgements

Models
Isabelle Schrauwen
Christine Bedell
Johnna Buttrick

I sincerely thank them for their inspiration and participation.
Yeah, I only hang out with hot chicks. Your jealousy is justified.

Literary
Me. Just me. All fucking me.
Naysayers gonna naysay.

Check out ChainsawAlice.com

Dangerous Worlds

Love & Chaos

Foreword

What is it?

Steampunk horror?
Victorian gore porn?
Fucked up fantasy?
Historical hentai?
YA parapornal romance?
Anachronistic splatterpunk erotica?

Yes! Yes! Yes! Yes! Meh. Yes!

The SICKEST steampunk book ever written!
Lots of killing and fucking in a past that never was.

What is the age of consent for a sentient anthropomorphic badger?

Is Alice an allegory for a woman's right to abortion?
Chainsaw. Pro-choice.
Sometimes a red sunset is just a red sunset.
Take what you want from this book. *wink*

But if you really think Alice's chainsaw is a misogynistic compensatory Freudian killboner you're probably going to fail your psych thesis. And you are stupid.

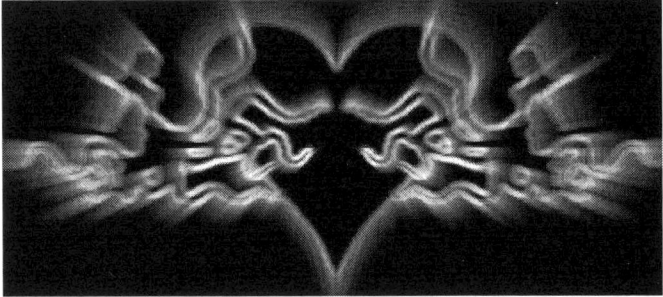

You haven't really lived until you've engaged in a drunken humping frenzy of furries, female cow skull demons, and cop cars. Sex on the dance floor. Iko iko!

Secret Breakfast Table of Contents

1. Rabbit Hole Down — 1
2. Dropping the Modified Kids off at the Pool — 8
3. Caucus Race and Long Tail — 12
4. There's Something in the Water — 16
5. The Failed Musician & the Girl w/ the Rusty Heart — 18
6. Avatar of the Meat God and the Looking Glass Map — 24
7. The First Unicorn — 30
8. Send me a Rabbit, Ritorubiru — 32
9. Advice from a Fractapillar — 39
10. Jack Fell Down — 46
11. Bar Fight at the Open Air Strip Club — 50
12. The Yellow King — 61
13. Pig and Pepper — 80
14. Mad Tea Party — 97
15. Battle Hookers "Action" Figures — 109
16. Ghoul Parade — 121
17. Killing is my Business. . .and Business is Good! — 126
18. World's Greatest Boss — 138
19. Thgink Teloiv — 143
20. Post Wartorn Depression — 147
21. My Knight in Stolen Armor — 150
22. Zuggernaut — 167
23. Party Smashers — 172

Shit's about to get weird.

Rabbit Hole
        Down
              - Chapter 1

    Outside the bank, sitting with her sister whom she normally has nothing to do with, Alice was beginning to get very tired. Once or twice she had peeped into the book her sister was reading, but the banal bibliogen said, "Look, Alice, this one has pictures," in a mocking tone. "You need to use this book." It was about good manners.
    There was no conversation, just orders. Alice did not like being given orders.
    She felt dopey and very sleepy. What a hot day. She sat considering the hearts of her own desires, when suddenly a white rabbit ran close to her.
    Of itself, there was nothing quite remarkable, but it does interfere with one's senses to hear a rabbit say to itself, "I was thinking about it very much! Was I was, if I were; am I, I? Oh well. Lateness. Time and tide."
    When she thought it over later, she should have wondered about it, but it happened to her that everything looked natural at the time. But, rabbit facts: They do not have waist coats, nor pocket watches to take out of them, but this one did. There was a flishflash, a surge of adventure. "After it!" She gave chase.
    It hippity-hop pippity-popped across the park and down a rabbit hole of rather largish size that was tucked away under a hedge. Hurrying after, Alice thought, "Was I was, in time only; back and forth, I should have known me." A time rhyme. She hadn't heard that since she was a child. The rabbit must be a chrononaut, the same as she.
    Given the world, never once down to another moment, she gave not a thought as to whether she would go *out of* again. Alice was not afraid to die. She had, in fact, done so several times. At least by laymen standards. Three times alone while fighting Captain Pruetta and her Uberian sky pirates while sailing perilously through the Rolocado Peaks. Getting knocked off the airship and smash landing at maximum velocity into a mountainside took a little bit more to

come back from, having been unable to slip sideways through time in a fastidious enough manner to avoid the impact.
Even when you know it is literally not your time to die, she really should be more careful.
In her headlong fiery pursuit, she found herself falling. Dipping and lifting, faster and slower, she felt quite giddy.
The hole was deep. Very. She tumbled bottoms up head over heels flip flop right side up again, and finally regained her center of balance. She fell very slowly. First, looking at the bottom, she tried to drop faster, but could not. A time trap!
"Perhaps I should slip my goggles on. Eye protection is very important regardless of velocity," Alice said. And she did so.
She bounced like a balloon as she gently drifted. She adjusted her dress as she floated past a looking glass. Having an odd buoyancy, her foot tapped the mirror and knocked it askew. It dropped and dipped down the rabbit hole, bumping the sides as it fell.

She looked around her and realized that the area was covered with bookshelves and cupboards filled with all sorts of exotic matter. She pulled out her jump map and looked it over. There were not supposed to be any temporal portals here, especially under a bush outside a bank in the middle of London. She took framed photos off of pegs here and there and placed them in her satchel.

She liked to collect things. One jar was labeled "ORANGE MARMALADE" but it was empty, a big disappointment for her.

There was quite an eclectic display of items. Silver slippers, a wolf suit, a Tumera Peppercorn voodoo doll kit, a set of ethereal chains (for catching ghosts) but no locks to be seen, a bent epee, a metal lunchbox with a picture of a laughing French skull stamped into the lid and the words "We are THE MISERABLE ONES" emblazoned across it, a broken nutcracker, a pair of pirate boots, a wooden snake with glowing eyes (luminous paint that one would think was made from firefly guts but it actually consists of pulverized bioluminescent cephalopod carcasses), and a shelf filled with cans of a precooked meat product of unknown origin with a green label that said "ROAST BEAST" but had no cartoonish picture of the actual animal to entice people to partake of its canned deliciousness.

A cricket sawing its legs inside a rotting jack o' lantern provided an eerie accompaniment to her descent. And there was glitter everywhere.

There were jars filled with various hard candies, but one different from the others particularly caught her eye. A jar of liquid darkness, to be precise. Something was bubbling on the inside but she could not tell the consistency of the contents. As she fumbled for it, the jar slipped her grasp and plummeted down the rabbit hole at a much greater pace than herself.

"After the collapse of such a waveform reality paradigm, it is assumed that you do not think anything about tumbling down the stairs!" thought Alice to herself. "How brave they'll think me at home, one and all! If I even fell from the top of the house, why, I would not say anything about it!" It was likely very high, that possibility. Alice's boredom had forced her to rethink her place in life. Her subconscious unhappiness had taken her someplace out of space, out of time, where rabbits wear waist coats and time does not fly, it falls! "Just keep telling yourself, 'It's all a dream.'"

Down, down, down. "Never remember comes at the end of the fall! I wonder. Miles I've fallen, by this time," she said aloud. "There is a need to get somewhere close to the center of the earth. Let us ponder. It would have to be 4000 miles down, I think. Advice?" she asked herself in the third person. "'We recommend that you stay above,' they would say. But then I wonder what Latitude or Longitude I have? Not to mention my Dropitude." Not being able to make heads nor tails of her location in relative space, Alice folded up her jump map and returned it to her satchel.

Currently, she began again. She was slipping into nonsense.

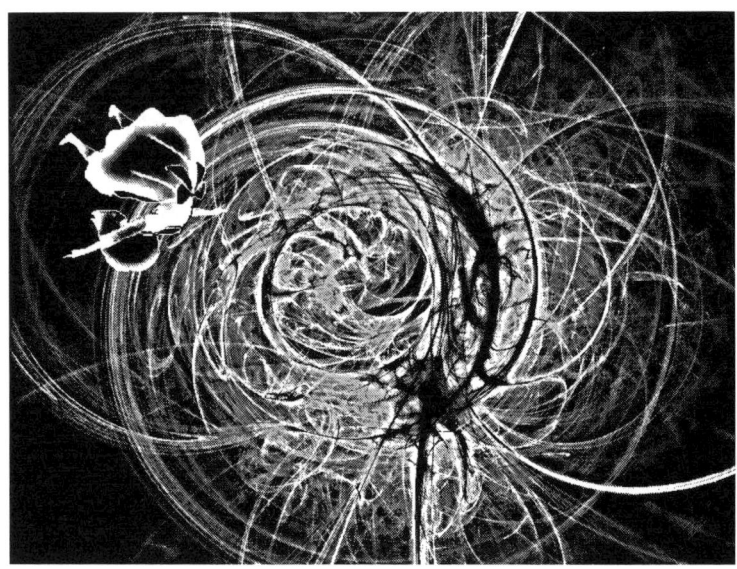

Down, down, down. She missed her cat. "Dinah, I hope they'll put your saucer of milk out at tea time. Dinah, my dear, even though the decrease, this indecent descent, is in here with me! I'm afraid, a mouse is not in the air out there, where there is a possibility that you will catch the bat, very, it's like a mouse, you know. However, the cat wonders aloud (in Alice's imagination), "I do not eat bats."
    She imagined walking hand in hand with Dinah now, "Dinah, do tell the truth to me, you ate a bat." Suddenly, thump! Thump! Down she came upon a heap of dried leaves and sticks, and the fall was over. There was a lingering dizziness. It took her a moment to refocus. A broken looking glass was beside her, the one she had toppled, and it had been splattered with a black viscous material.
    Alice was not hurt and she jumped to her feet in an instant. She lifted her goggles. There was darkness above her and a long passage in front. She saw the white rabbit and boy was he in a hurry! Listening, it said, "Oh, whiskers and my ears," as it turned the corner, "there's no moment to be lost. I'm just in time for. . ."

When she turned the corner, she was not close behind him. She saw no rabbit, but found herself in a hall, lit by lamps hanging from the roof, long, low. "This is like reading bad crime dramas," Alice thought to herself as her perception of reality began to distort. Jump lag. It happens periodically after passing through a time warp.

There was a golden key on a glass table. Alice tried to unlock all the doors along the hall, but alas, none would open for the key was too small. She returned the key to the table.

Every door was locked tight. Alice walked between them sadly. Behind a meager curtain she found a diminutive door she had not seen before. She opened it and tried to squeeze through, but to no avail.

"Oh, would-be-want-to!" her friend Kano would say. And that she was too fat to fit, because he always teased her about everything. He was kind of an asshole. She didn't know why she was friends with him.

She found a crumpled up handbill. It said, "WOLFCO" at the top with a picture of a menacing wolf's head and the words "You'll huff and puff" underneath. She saw no reason to keep the vague advertisement and tossed it aside.

She noticed a bottle that was not here before, certainly. A bottle of Most. Most hopeful? Most delightful? Most dreadful? There was a paper label attached to the neck, printed on it in anycase words of drinking, "ME, in the beautiful." Not uppercase, not lowercase, but anycase; because they are words, usually of advice, that can be used in any case.

If you drink a lot from a bottle marked, "Poison--Sooner or Later" it will burn like a red-hot poker, eventually. And that would be most disagreeable. Alice very seldom agreed with herself, yet alone with poison.

However, Alice plunged in and tasted it. She concluded very soon that it was not poison, unless it was poison of the Later variety. In which case, she would find out later. It tasted like bacon butter muffintruffs, the kind Mister Tesla used to make with his coiler grill. He always said they were easy to bake. She would see him down at the park every Sunday morning, breaking up the muffinos (muffins for ruffians, mustachio optional) and feeding the birds. Alice didn't think the bacon was good for them, but he was the scientist. She was the only one who recognized him. He would never tell her why he made those secret trips to London from New York.

How she missed him.

"Feel what curiosity strong!" Alice said, "I must be blocked as a telescope."
And she certainly was. The elixir caused her to shrink down to 10 inches high; just the right size to go through the small door and into the nice garden now.
First, however, she waited a few minutes to make sure was not going to shrink any further. When she arrived at the door, she found another smaller door further inside. One that would surely accommodate the little golden key; which she had put back on the table. The legs of the table were too slippery to climb. The poor thing rubbed her eyes and plopped down crisscross apple sauce. She

was very upset with herself. And adapting to this new place after the time jump was giving her a headache. The words she was thinking and saying were coming out backwards, backwords; like a reflection in a looking glass, everything was reversed. She was clearly beside herself, figuratively.

    Alice lost her balance as she tried to stand. She fell and scraped against a small glass box that was lying under the table. "My ass hurts," Alice said, rubbing it. She opened the glass box and inside it was a petite cake with the words "I AM IN IT" on it. "If I grow big," thought Alice, I can reach the key. If I grow small, I can creep under the door, so I'll get to the garden either way. I do not care which happens!"

    She ate a nibble, and said anxiously, "Which one? Any way." She was very surprised to find that she was still the same size. Sure, which typically occurs when you eat cake with no distinctive warnings or curious ingredients; but nothing. It seemed foolish to go on in a common way, her dull and very Alice life. But things happen out-of-way, in places like this. And not so much in the way you would expect. Out of hand, and certainly out of her mind.

    She finished off the cake.

Who the fuck is making all these cakes that alter reality?
I think you know.
Try the insanity, it's delicious!

Dropping the Modified Kids off at the Pool - Chapter 2

"More and more strange and increasingly bizarre!" cried Alice. She was quite surprised that while she speaks good English, she seemed to have forgotten how. "The largest telescope so far like spread I am now! Good-bye, feet!" It looked like they almost disappeared, when she looked at her feet, they were getting so far off. "Oh, my poor little feet, but what of your shoes and stockings now, dears? I can not be sure! I am so far away and I am having trouble myself. You must manage the best way.

"But I must be kind to them," thought Alice, "or walk down the street probably they want to go do not! Let me see: I will give them a new pair of boots for their annual Christmas." Alice realized that she was having a discussion with her feet. This was not acceptable.

Alice began to grow larger and larger.

She was planning how to soliloquy and manage it. She thought, "How interesting, sending gifts to one's feet! What strange directions I have taken, and all at the same time. Well, what nonsense I'm talking about!"

She collisioned...no, the word is collisiofrissioned, with the roof of the hall. It means to collide in such a way and at such an angle that you not only bump your head but you get a good friction rub burn as well. The kind which is severe enough to take off a layer of skin. Then you're picking scab pieces out of your hair for a week. Fortunately it wasn't that bad.

She was high, nine feet or more now in fact. She took the key and hurried off to the little door.

Poor Alice! She looked through the keyhole with one eye and saw a lovely garden lying beyond. She unlocked the door and opened it as far as it would go. But she was too big to fit through the door again.

She noticed that she was sitting in a large pool. It was blood! She had apparently cut her ass on the glass box when she fell upon it. When she grew again it greatly opened the gash. The pool had reached halfway across the corridor and had a depth of about 3 inches. That's a lot of blood.

After some time had elapsed, she heard a pattering of small feet in the distance. She rubbed her eyes and saw someone coming in a hurry. It was the White Rabbit, dressed beautifully in his waist coat and pocket watch, carrying a large white fan in one hand and wearing an interesting pair of electroshock gloves, like something dear old Tesla would have concocted. The Easter beaster was muttering to himself as he came trotting along in a rush, "Duke, Duchess! Oh! If you've kept the waiting time too long...savage! She's savage, I tell you."

Alice tried to get his attention. The rabbit started violently and scurried away in the dark. He was so filled with fright that he dropped his fan in the excitement.

"Dear, dear, this will not do at all," she said to herself. The bottom half of her dress was soaked in blood. It was beginning to dry and becoming very tacky on her hands and body. "How strange, all things this day! And that yesterday I went on just as usual. I wonder if I changed in the night? Let me think: When I got up this morning, was I the same? I think that I can remember feeling a little different almost. If I am not the same 'who I am' in the world, the next question is, 'Are you?' But contrariwise, that should be the first question when asked to oneself. So I am surely a different person, beyond the standard change given the passage of time, which does not apply to me because of my chronokinetic abilities. Oh, it's a great puzzle!" She began to think over all the children she knew who had been modified.

Mabel? Ada? Kano? Crockett? Hmm. They still seemed themselves, except with the addition of their mechanical parts and limbs.

She tried to recite the multiplication table but it became exponentially difficult. She tried to recite one of her limerickal lessons:

To improve the tail shining, how little crocodile, doth pour the water of the Nile River on a scale of gold all!

How he spread the nail of his neatly merrily, how welcome a little fish with smile chin gently, it seems to be laughing!

"I'm sure that is not word appropriate. It keeps coming out like some sort of elite language known only by difference engineers; which would explain why I feel so different." Alice took another swig from the bottle and finished it off. As she did this, she began to shrink again. There was a splash at her legs and she slipped! She was up to her chin in blood.

"Oh, had I not bled so much!" Alice swam about. "To be drowning in a pool of one's own blood, certainly, it is peculiar. But it becomes the thing. Everything is strange to Japan."

At that time, she heard a sloshing about in the pool a little far away (not tremendously far away; not far, far away at all). She thought it must be a hippopotamus or walrus at first, but then she remembered how small she was now. She saw that it was only a mouse that had slipped in like her.

"Would it be any use at all to speak to this mouse?" Alice thought. "I'm very tired! I have never done such a thing before." She tried to speak to it, but it did not respond.

"Perhaps it does not speak English." So she tried some broken French.

The mouse squeaked with fear, "I do not like cats!"

Alice was trying to explain about her cat Dinah, but to no avail.

"Fuck off! and your cat!" it squirked.

"I will not indeed!" Alice said in a hurry, best to change the subject of conversation. But the mouse ignored her and swam away.

There was a creature of curiosity here, a Dodo, and a pretty good size crowd of birds and animals that had also fallen into the pool of blood. Higher is where to go. It was time. With Alice leading the way, all parties swam through the blood flood to find shore.

Caucus Race and Long Tail - Chapter 3

Birds with feathers dirty by being dragged, and animals, cross, wet, uncomfortable, drip-drop-drooping, fur clingy and matted - a strange assemblage at the bank of the sanguine pool.

They had been blood mud slinging.

The crimson creek flowed down the hall, through the door, and out into the garden.

"Ahem! Ready, all?" asked Dodo. "Mouse has an important air," he said with a sarcastic tone. "This is the driest I know. Round all of silence, if you please! William the Conqueror, which is supported by the Pope. The cause of Morcar and Edwin, which is filed as wanting a leader immediately, in English, was from and hitherto fore accustomed to conquest and usurpation of many in the second half, Northumbria and Mercia. Earls of..."

"Wow! Raleigh tremble!" Alice said.

"Is that like the truffle shuffle?" asked Dodo.

"No, no, most certainly not," answered Potoo. "That's in East Carolina, where Kurtulu sleeps. There's a memorial bench that says, 'Kurtulu slept here.' Probably on one of those invalid waterbeds though. He's a heavy sleeper, you know."

"I beg your pardon! Mouse frown," said Mouse, but not very politely, as his action mimicked his statement. "You did speak?" he directed his ire at Alice. "I thought you were fucking off. And you can address me by my full proper name, Long Tail. That is, if I was talking to you and you weren't busy fucking off. So, now, go fuck off somewhere. Get to fucking. Off, that is. Get to fucking off."

"Not I of!" the Lory said in a hurry, cutting off Alice's response to the mouse's rudeness.

"What about Merica?" Duck asked.

"Does she have the wonders yet?" one wise Owl asked.

"No, I don't see the wonder in her. At least not yet," said the Raven, "but don't quote me. Perhaps a few sips of dandelion wine would do wonders for her.

"I wonder," questioned the European Swallow, "what about the prizes? And where is the King of Milk?"

"But who is to provide the prizes?" the Chorus Considerable voiced, completely ignoring the kingly business. Which is a shame, because the type of milk for a caucus race is very important. Regular? Almond? Coconut? Chocolate? Snozzberry?

Dodo said, pointing at Alice, "Why, she! Prize! Prize!"

They began picking and pecking at her.

"Oo! Ow! Stop it!" she cried, fending off their encroaching aggressions. "Stop it, or you'll be sorry!"

"It's all her fault. Back in the hall, the whole mess," said Long Tail. "Let's go to law fury: I will prosecute you - Come on, I would not be negative. We, you," he wiggled his nose at Alice, "must have a trial. This morning, really."

"Yesterday he holds his peace, today he won't shut up," interjected Goose.

"I love law furies," said Possum.

The mouse continued unabated, "What is your relation to the defendant, to yourself, that is? To the latest version ispo facto upso downo, in such a test, dear. And there is no judge or jury. That will waste the breath of us. I'll be judge, I'll be jury. Law fury! Law fury! I look at the cause of the whole, and would blame you to death."

    Still they poked, pulled, and prodded at her. Points of blood dotted her skin from the claw and beak penetrations.

    "You would judge me?" asked Alice, now clearly losing her patience. "In truth, you're all just a bunch of buzzards, scavengers, gadflies, unnecessary carrion crawlers. Muckrakers. Vitspitters. Filthfeeders. You want prizes?" They all shook their heads affirmatively and looked at her expectantly. "I have a prize for you." She pulled a large folding knife out of her pinafore pocket. "The harvest feast has come early. Time to carve the birds."

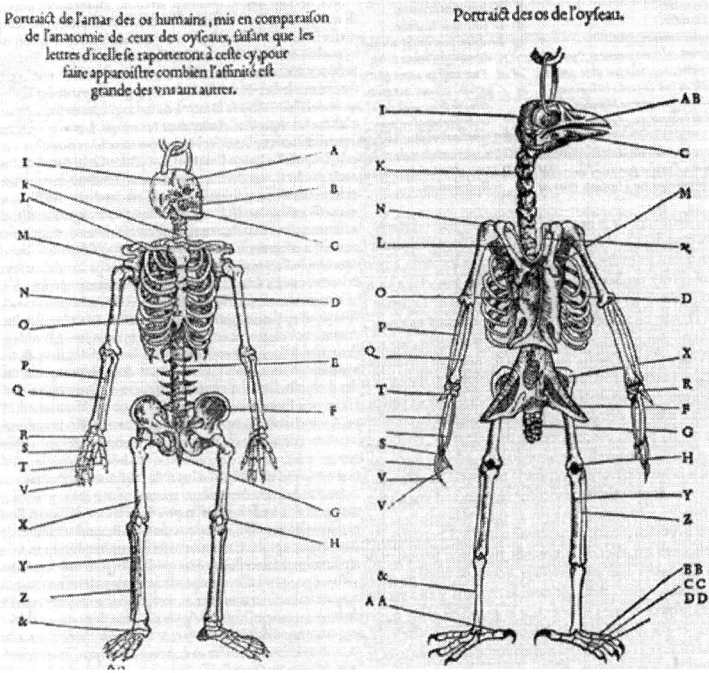

    She grabbed Dodo first, as he was the largest and closest of the fowl beasts. She clamped his beak so that he could not hook her with it, then she sliced straight across his long neck. Blood rained down more and more as his head flailed, stretching the gaping gullet wound.

    She twisted his head and flung him to the ground. With a final burbling of blood, Dodo was dead.

"You're next, mouse."

Long Tail had been stuck to the spot in fright and disbelief. She scruffed him and pulled him close. "You were a backbiter. Now you'll be a facespiter," Alice said as she moved her hand from his nape to his nose and held tight. With her other hand she used the knife to slice through the tough cartilage of his pointy snout. As she neared the end of her task she pulled the nose the rest of the way off by its spindly remaining skin.

Blood gushed everywhere. Long Tail tried to staunch the flow but to no avail.

Alice flicked his nose back at him. It bounced off his coat and onto the ground. She grabbed him by the scruff again, "C." She held up the pocket knife so that he could see it glimmer in the sunlight, "A." She stabbed him square in the throat and then up into his brain, "T." She pulled the knife out and let him drop. "Cat."

She turned toward the other animals who were cowering and clustering together, "Who else wants a fucking prize?"

Alice did a quick grab-n-stab to the rest of the group. A few managed to trigger the "RUN MOTHER FUCKER!" button on their fight-or-flight internal mechanisms and escaped while she slaughtered those who had remained behind. Sorry Possum, it didn't work.

Alice was soon left alone.

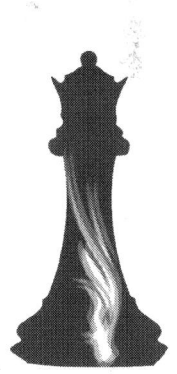

She noticed a blue chess piece amidst the red carnage. It was a queen. There was a creature painted on one side but Alice could not quite make out what it was supposed to be. Probably some localized fantastical monstrosity. Never leave anything open to artistic interpretation.

There's Something in the Water - Chapter 4

Alice made her way out of the garden, across the small hills and the freshly mown lawn. She stopped by a babbling brook and waded in to wash the blood from her dress. She pulled off her clothes and scrubbed the clotted mess clean. The moving water diffused the blood and washed it downstream.

Perhaps it was the constant altering of her physical size, but she felt giddy. She had jumped through many a time tunnel before, but never one like this. She wasn't just giddy, she was feeling aroused.

She looked about and made sure no one was around. The brook was sunken below the bank so she could not be seen unless the spectator was at its edge. She tossed her clothing into the grass to dry.

Alice started touching herself. Slowly, at first. The cool water felt good on her skin. It had been awhile since the last time.

She started masturbating faster and faster and faster. The water churned furiously. Until finally, with a stuttering whimper, she reached orgasm. She fell back in the water, satisfied, and pressed herself against the high bank. Nothing like a little stress reliever on a topsy turvy day such as this. There were many, many benefits to her chronokinetic powers.

Alice retrieved her clothes after a tranquil repose. They were dry enough to put back on and continue her journey, wherever it led. She did not notice the female head peek over the embankment as she left. It was a mermaid with a mechanical arm, but the appendage was constructed from grown and shaped coral, a lost limb replaced by another symbiotic lifeform. If only she could love again, "Deeper, blacker, my heart is like a sharkskin."

She was corking a large decanter she had just filled with water from the brook. To what end we do not know, but for some sinister purpose it must be.

Her eyes glowed with an indigo intensity, "I've not tasted such power," she said, and began levitating out of the water when Alice passed over the nearby hill and could not see her. She flew through the air in a swimming motion and was gone.

The Failed Musician and the Girl with the Rusty Heart - Chapter 5

"You are a wonderful distraction from
　　　　　this misery called life." --Seisrush Ob

　　　　Alice came to a small hoodoo with a young girl sitting atop it. She was gently weeping. How she managed to climb up the faery chimney rock was unknown, as it was very steep and covered in moss. Her tattered white dress had elegant but novice embroidery covering it, betraying that she was trying to be something that she was not. You can't spin a queen's habit from a haversack. "Never stop reaching for the stars, my dear," Alice silently advised the weeping girl.

There was a man in merry-andrew regalia at the base of the hoodoo playing a huluhu. He did not play the spike fiddle very well. But he sang with all the passion in the world.

He sang:

Crush, crush! Crash, crash!
Crush, crush! Crash, crash!
Crush, crush! Crash, crash!
You know my love wasn't built to last

Failed starts, rusted hearts, stolen tarts, broken parts
Joker's queen, new machine, love unseen, a little boy's dream

Sadness is madness, emotion is corrosion
Sadness is madness, emotion is corrosion

Crush, crush! Crash, crash!
Crush, crush! Crash, crash!
Crush, crush! Crash, crash!
You know my love wasn't built to last

Shadowy wings, impossible things, magic rings, mimsy kings
Unbirthday parades, empty accolades, caterwauling serenades, boisterous escapades

Sadness is madness, emotion is corrosion
Sadness is madness, emotion is corrosion

It's not the thought that counts

When he came to the end, the young girl said, "Thank you. That was beautiful. Will you play it again?"
"For you, anything," he replied.

A muscular man, bald but with scraggly sideburns and a bushy mustache, wearing only a pair of Turkish trousers, walked past Alice cracking his knuckles. He had a tattoo on his upper left arm of a steer's head with a dollar sign where the bull's eye would be; a moneytaur, a dollar bull. He had a wicked sneer and an air of violence about him. He was intending to do harm to the poor heartbroken duo.

"What are you going to do?" Alice asked him.
"Shut up, girl!" he replied. That was all the justification she needed.
"Excuse your exclamation?" Alice said with an implied, "What the fuck did you just say?"
"I said, *shut up*, unless you want to get hurt, too."
"So, you're going to assault these innocent people. And if I get in your way, me as well?"
"Yes. Try and stop me," he said, madness in his eyes.
Alice gave him three rabbit punches to the kidney and spun him around. She unleashed a barrage of stomach punches to the big man--rock around the clock. She sidestepped to the left and continued her flurry of fists of fury and moved in a clockwise pattern around the kooky cowboy. His body flailed from the hits but he remained standing.
Alice came full circle around the bully. His midsection hurt

all over, he didn't know where to hold his stomach at in a vain attempt to ease the pain. "Are you ready for the Accelerator?" she asked rhetorically. The motion of her fist blurred through space-time as she delivered a chronokinetically powered uppercut which sent him flying several feet in the air. He landed on his back with a thud. He was out cold.

Alice dusted off her hands, "That's that," and walked over to the wonky warbler. "So what's this all about?" she asked him.

"The man you just saved us from is one of the enforcers of the Knave of Hearts. The Jack, that one-eyed bastard, has been experimenting on the people of our land. He kidnaps them and uses his weird science to replace their organs or body parts." The sorrowful songster looked up toward his love, "He has taken my sweet Patina's heart and replaced it with a mechanical one. Only now, it is rusting. The more she feels the more her emotions corrode it from the inside out. Loving me is killing her, so she has retreated up this spire."

"Don't worry; what was your name?" Alice asked.

"Joe the Strumfounded Fool."

"I'm Alice. Joe, don't worry." She yelled up to Patina, "I'm going to fix this. It's what I do. I fix things." The weeping girl gave her a small smile and nodded in thanks. "Love is the greatest madness," Alice said. "And I will fight for it in all its guises."

Alice dragged the unconscious cowboy into a shady copse. There were wild grapes growing about the small wooded area. She used some of the vines to bind him and had a delicious snack of the fresh fruit as she did so. She fashioned a noose, tightened it around his neck, threw it over the low branch of a nearby tree, then tied it back into the noose. When he wakes, the more he struggles the more he will hang himself. He had just enough rope.

She smashed some of the grapes and used the juice to stain a message on his chest, "BE NICER."

Alice found a leaflet tacked to a tree. Another WOLFCO ad, no slogan this time. "Subtle," Alice thought. "Familiarize the population with your name and image, but don't reveal your true self. Get them talking about you, gossiping. All wrapped up in sheep's clothing."

Avatar of the Meat God and the Looking Glass Map - Chapter 06

    A group of dead men were littered across the road as Alice came around the gently sloping bend. They wore white tunics with red diamonds on them, as if dressed like playing cards. Another, dressed in noble garb, had a "J" on his royal whites. Ah, the Jack of Diamonds, Alice realized. Dead also. She wondered what kind of game they must have been playing, and perhaps they should not have played with stakes so high.
    A naked man stood over the Jack. He was the pinnacle of physical actualization. His muscles were like chiseled stone, stronger than any normal human could achieve. His buttocks was tight and lithe. His hair was perfect.

    A knight in sharply angled armor stood beside him. He wielded a large sword with a triangular blade. There was a strange symbol on his chest plate. It was a stylized W in black over a red pyramid (or an inverted V), like an off kilter argyle. Alice felt like she should recognize it, but could not place its origin or allegiance.
    The naked man's penis extended like a prehensile tentacle. Its urethral opening was a toothless maw and began devouring the Jack's junk! The fallen card's lower torso had become slurry-like and the trunk-dick was siphoning off the flesh. Alice could see the viscera throb down the shaft of the sucking cock and into el perfecto's body. He raised his hand and shouted, "In the name of Snae Varath, God of Meat, your debt is paid."
    "Really, Mazziel, do you have to be so melodramatic?" asked the knight sarcastically.

"The theatrics help keep things interesting," the aliment angel replied. "Many of the higher stratum consider lower vibrational worlds such as this to be contemptuous. I love them. The potential for these meat suits is nearly limitless. It is a pity that so many of them take it for granted. Or fight over pigmentation. They all bleed red."

"Those aether planar beings think their paradigm shift doesn't stink. But remember, not many have the abilities you do here. You are, after all, the avatar of a bio god."

"And do you know my response to that?" he asked as his serpentine penis raised up and pointed at the knight--then it belched.

Both rolled with laughter.

Alice approached them without fear. She did not expect trouble, and was unsure if she could take both at once should the encounter escalate to an armed conflict, as they were obviously veterans in the combat arts, but that would neither deter her nor intimidate her.

"Godly, knightly," she said to each respectively.

They both looked at her curiously. "Hello, young lady," said the knight. "I apologize if my companion's lack of clothing embarrasses you."

"I don't," said the naked angel. "The human form is a beautiful biological machine. Each one is unique in its shape, ability, and aesthetic appeal which only serves to aid in your entanglement as a species and your advancement as a planetary unit. None should be ashamed."

"Nothing I haven't seen before," Alice smiled. The knight guffawed.

"I'll bet there's one thing you haven't seen before," the meat avatar said, pondering.

"No, no, no. None of that now. I think she's already seen enough of YOUR abilities today," said the knight, "and I have no desire to see anymore of them myself." He laughed again.

"Very well," the exposed extrovert replied. "And if I may introduce myself, I am Mazziel, avatar of Snae Varath the Meat God. I would offer my hand in greeting, but as you can tell, my divinity and the work I do for him is rather messy. And this is my temporary temporal associate, Andres Zachson, warp knight."

"Ahh, now I recognize your symbol," she said. "We are

similarly 'employed' one might say. I am Alice Wardell, chrononaut." Both men bowed while Alice curtsied.

"Yes, this is quite the strange land, is it not?" Andres said.

"Indeed. Even the minor horological anomalies still have my head spinning," Alice said.

"And may we be of any assistance to you this day?" Mazziel asked. "I do not wish to seem abrupt, but I do have pressing unfinished business to attend to."

"A million years of nothing to do and now he's too busy to stop and chat," Andres said. "An anticelestial's work is never done."

"As you yourself alluded to, this entire place is a mad house."

Alice queried, "I am in need of someone with expertise in automatons. And if you might know the location of the Jack of Hearts. He and I need to discuss his tinker habits."

"Ah, Jack-o's up to no good again I see," Mazziel said.

You'll run into him soon enough, of that you can be sure," Andres added. "Unfortunately I do not know anyone of the technical sort in these parts."

"Nor I. Do you still have that map?" Mazziel asked him. "The one you got from the blossom possum."

"Yes, I believe I do," Andres replied as he rummaged through several pouches. "Aha! Here it is." He handed it to Alice.

"I don't understand. These notes beside the different locations look like they are in my handwriting, but how can that be? You have just handed this to me and I have never been to any of these places."

"It is a looking glass map. Many things here, like logic, time, metropolitan thinking, brillig, certain cakes, and continental drift theory to name several, which is more than a few but less than a slew, all operate in reverse or with very different and/or distorted results. You mentioned feeling disjointed after your initial arrival here; that is why."

"So, how do I read it, then?" Alice asked.

"Normally you read a map and then decide where to go. A looking glass map shows where you will go when you read it."

"So it's a probability map. Because nothing is predetermined and time is an energy which can be altered like any other. I *am* a chrononaut. I haven't found a physical world yet that could command my actions."

"Yes. Path of least resistance, wave form collapse upon

observation, Schrödinger's Guide to Weird Roadside Attractions, etcetera. And look here!" he said pointing to the map, "Looks like you'll be running into the Jack of Hearts very soon. But you are right, you still have free will. You could sit down right here and never leave this spot again. That's your appanage."
"No. I think I'll go with the flow."
"Time keeps on slipping into the future."
"Two minutes to midnight."
"Once upon."
"Nostalgia is stagnation."
"Flies."
"Is money."
"Out of."
"Ahead of."
"Tea."
"All in good."
"Time enough at last."
Alice smiled, "Time enough at last."

"Clock-knockers," Mazziel said.

She sine waved goodbye and went on her way.

Alice was walking and trying to make heads or tails of the looking glass map when she nearly ran into a woman who was carrying a massive bundle of baskets on her shoulders. She did not seem to be burdened or bothered by her load.

"This map is useless to someone like me," Alice thought and folded it up and put it away.

"Excuse me," Alice said. "I wasn't paying attention."

"Not to worry. Tell me, are you a wanderer or a traveler?"

"Both. I am an adventurer."

"Exceptional! I am Pandora. And you are?"

"Alice."

They shook hands. "It is a pleasure to meet you," Pandora said.

"And you as well."

"As you can see," she turned slightly to display her bale and made a silly 'duh' face, "I have baskets. Would you like one? They are filled with, surprises."

"Surprises? Like what?"

"Not even I know. That is the fantastic nature of things! You never know what's inside until you look."

"Alas, I have no money." The reason Alice had tagged along to the bank with her sister. "And I have nothing to trade."

"Oh, my dear, everyone has something to give. Many just

don't know the value of the things they have. Do you have a smile to trade? To give? To share?"

Alice instinctively smiled.

"You see, a fair trade indeed," Pandora said, who reciprocated the gesture. "Mine are always free. No strings attached. It makes my heart sad when so many cannot allow themselves to receive simple acts of kindness. Attention is a quantum hug. And we all need and crave that. It is our human nature."

"Yes, I understand," Alice said, smiling wider.

"Today is your schrödawn. Your life will be as full or as empty as you desire. Now, pick a basket. Find your wonder!"

"I am a schrödawner. I like the sound of that." Alice walked around her looking the bundle up and down. So many sizes and styles.

Alice picked a small, square, lidded basket.

"What's inside?" Pandora asked.

"Let us find out." Alice opened the lid and pulled out a bear figurine made of malachite.

"It will protect you in your travels, as well as your wanderings," said the belle of baskets.

Alice thanked her, affixed the nacelle to her satchel, and then they bid each other goodbye.

THE FIRST UNICORN - 007

There was a young woman sitting beneath a tree by the side of the pathway, her hair and eyes were a stark violet in color. She wore red armor and a morning star lay next to her. A helmet shaped like a horse head was on its side several yards away as if it had been tossed there in frustration. She had a spiraling horn growing from the top front of her head. She slumped hard against the weeping willow and had a perplexed look on her face.
"Are you lost?" Alice asked.
"Locationally, no. D'etre-ly, yes."
"You have lost your, beingness?" Alice questioned.
"Yes. I am inbetween. I am not fully of any one world."
"Please explain."

"This morning, I was so proud. For I was but a simple pawn when I awoke, but then I became a knight. The first in my family."

"A great honor then, indeed."

"Yes, verily. But I was a red knight. And as you can see," she pulled her fingers through her hair and presented it, "I am no longer a Red Chessian. I am, Violet."

"Are you part blue blood?" Alice asked.

"No. My family has always been red. Color mixing is frowned upon within our society. Secondary colors are shunned and ostracized. And there has never been a Violet Kingdom, nor violet people to fill it. I don't understand what has happened."

"Were you driven away by your own kind?"

"No. I fled before anyone could see. I have heard of faery Chessians before, those born with or given special abilities, which is what I have become. The horn would signify that I am not a knight at all, but a unicorn. Some would call me a knightmare. I don't fit in. I don't belong anywhere."

"Well, my name is Alice, and I'm a bit 'locationally' out of sorts myself. Would you like to walk with me for awhile?"

"As a knight, or, as a knightly unicorn, I will of course accompany you on your journey. I am Dame Desultoria, but you can call me Sultori."

So they walked together and Sultori told Alice about the Chess people and the various hazards of these lands. Alice enquired after someone who could help Patina but the Violet Knight did not know anyone. They came to a forested neighborhood of cottages.

"The animals who live here are a touch busybodyish, but they are otherwise a nice enough flock of folk," Sultori said.

"Then I shall thank you for your escort and take my leave," Alice said. "I hope you find your place in the world."

"As do I. As do I."

It was the White Rabbit again, trotting back slowly, looking about anxiously as though he had lost something. He had changed out of his waistcoat and was wearing a tunic covered in a motley heart pattern and a royal ruff. He was also carrying a small announcing trumpet that had a heart flag attached to it. He muttered, "As I went! Oh my dear leg! Oh my fur beard! The more ferrets ferret, the more things stay the same. Can I, where I wonder, to have dropped it? The Duchess will. . ."

Alice realized that he must be looking for his fan which he dropped, and was now lost, in the pool of blood.

When he saw her, the rabbit called Alice in an exasperated tone of voice, "What are you doing here? Why, Mary Ann. Run this moment home and fetch my monogrammed fan! Now, quick!"

He was obviously upset at the loss of the fan, or at the thought of what this Duchess would do at the loss of the fan, so Alice did not correct the mistaken identity. And she liked rabbits, generally, so she ignored his demanding demeanor and decided to help the little guy instead.

She came upon a small house that was neat, with a bright brass plate on the door with the engraving "W. RABBIT" on it. Alice entered without knocking and began rummaging through the house in search of the fan. Small furniture filled the home. Too many throw pillows left no room to sit anywhere, thus defeating the purpose of either the furniture or the pillows. There was a gift bag from Wolfco in the kitchen, its contents of teas and sample jars of flarmalade had been spread out across the table.

No one really knew what flarmalade was. The label simply stated that it was "FLARMALADE - fabulous flavorlous deliciousness" but did not mention what the actual flavor was. Alice opened a jar and dipped her finger in it, "Hmmm, I'd say it tastes like allberry seraphood cake," then closed it.

After searching for a few tick-tocks, she found the fan and placed it in her pocket. She also came across a small bottle next to the looking glass on the vanity table. The label, this time, read "Do not drink the words. ME is there." She still uncorked it and put it to her lips, "I know it was confirmed that the fun stuff happens every time you drink something," Alice said to herself (author's note: I think Alice is developing a drinking problem).

Before she had even drank half the bottle she found her head pressed against the ceiling. "Quite enough - it is it," Alice said. "I cannot get out the door. I hope I shall not grow any more. This will not do. You would think I was drinking myself pretty." She put the bottle in her pinafore pocket.

Oh! It was too late to want! She had grown to the size of a giant. She curled one arm up and put the other one out the window. "What will become of me?"

Now, for Alice, it was only a little bottle of magic, but it had a very full effect. She that could not get the wonders so far is very uncomfortable still; she felt unhappy. And she wondered about "the wonders" the Owl and Raven had been discussing. Was it wonderful? Or ironic.

"It was pleasanter at home, not in size growth is always #1. The rabbit hole, it was good if not for the down-down-drop. Still! I know my curiosity is strong, but this is ridiculous. I wonder what is happening to me. I read faery tales when it is called for, but it never had a plot twist of this manner. And I'm right in the middle of one! I shall have to write down my adventures, should I ever get home. This is not how I want my story to end.

"They'll call me One-Way Comfort. Boys and blowjobs, won't you ever learn. I'll be able to give, but I'll be too big to get. Oh, you foolish Alice. Oh, I do not like it. The lessons of old women."

One would think that romantic incompatibilities would be the least of her worries.

"Mary Ann! Mary Ann!" came the White Rabbit's voice from outside. "Fetch my fan this moment!"

Alice shifted and knocked part of the roof off. Thatch and wooden support beams crashed down and smashed the cucumber garden fence. She heard Rabbit squeal in terror, "A land whale! A killer land whale! In my house! Get out of my house, whale!"

"Don't you know better than to say that to a woman?" Alice bellowed from inside the house.

"Go back to Stupid Cat City where you came from!" Whitey was not very good with insults. She heard him talking to someone else but could not make out what he was saying.

"That's it," Alice said. "I tried to help you, and this is how you treat me? I don't care about not damaging your house anymore." She smashed through the wall and rolled out of the crumbling cottage.

Standing next to the White Rabbit was a horned lizard with a samurai sword.

"There it is, Ritorubiru! Like I said it was!" the rabbit exclaimed and jostled the lizard, pricking his paw; luckily his electrogloves where thick enough to protect him.

"It is most fortunate that I was passing by, Rabbit. Your luck stands. I will dispose of this beast for you."

"Thank you, okashirasaurus, boss lizard," the White Rabbit said, bowed, then continued, "I must go to see the queen. I am late."

"Yes, go, I shall avenge your cucumbers. Inform the queen I shall return shortly."

The rabbit pulled out a snuff box, took a hit, tweaked his ears, and was off like a shot.

Alice eyed the little lizard. Little in comparison to her, that is. But he was a giant himself in comparison to the other creatures of this place. The horns extending from his back were like blades themselves. A closer look showed many of his scales were sloughing off his body. He was not shedding a skin, it actually looked gangrenous and melty. Something bad was going on inside of him.

"Always aspire to something greater than yourself, like killing giants," Ritorubiru said as he charged at Alice, sword aloft. He squirted a stream of noxious blood from his left eye as he did so in an attempt to blind Alice. She put up her hand and blocked the stream. And with a swift kick she punted him down the road.

A crowd of other birds and animals had gathered to watch the battle. They began throwing stones at her. A young girl wearing a witch's outfit that was much too large for her, a hand-me-down perhaps, the poor secondhand witch, sat on the brick fence surrounding the yard, "You animals are not nice," she chastised, "Shoo! Shoo! Go away!" but they would not listen.

"Why, you little. . ." Alice almost lost her temper again. "I should splat every last one of you." As she opened her mouth, one of the lucky rocklobbers landed a direct hit in the back of her throat. She gagged for a moment, then swallowed it. She realized that it was not a stone at all, but a stale cake. One of those changing cakes. She shrank to their level.

Ritorubiru was walking vehemently back up the road. Alice realized that her pocket knife would be of little use against a samurai sword. She needed to find a better weapon.

"The tool shed! Of course!" Alice declared, seeing it as she looked around for something to defend herself with against the oncoming lethal lizard.

She went to the rabbit-sized shed and gave the door a running kick. This busted off the cheap lock which was supposed to keep out thieves. It did hurt her foot somewhat. These thin-soled bar shoes would have to go.

Alice went in and rummaged about the tiny shed. *thud* "Ow, damn!" came a muffled exclamation. She had bumped her head on the low ceiling. "This whole height-forsaken place needs remodeling!" A terrible engine revved and roared from within, and with a riotous yelling, kicking, cutting, and smashing the shed was demolished, now nothing more than a pile of debris and firewood.

"You lack focus, little blonde thing," Ritorubiru said lifting his sword and taking a fighting stance.

Alice emerged from the dust cloud holding a wicked chainsaw; it was shiny, oiled, and growling. She began wielding it in an infinity pattern. As she did the blade seemed to spin faster and faster. A visible wave of energy emanated from it. Alice was using her chronokinetic power to deadly extreme.

The weight of the chainsaw strained and burned the muscles in her arms. But she liked the feel of it in her hands as the blade accelerated beyond terrestrial temporal limitations. She let up on the engine and said, "Alright, Sharp And Pointy, time to die."

Alice pulled the trigger and the chainsaw screamed to life. She swung it in an ever-widening figure eight. Ritorubiru stood his ground as she advanced.

"This is a jakoto katana. Forged 1000 years ago by Samurhino Hikareru. Your death will be an honor and your name will be added to the lineage of those killed by it. I will weep for you and sing the dirge of my people to ease your journey to the next world."

He was stalling, waiting for a momentary lag in her swing so that he could find a vulnerable opening and strike. Alice knew this.

Mid swing she turned full around and let the momentum of the motion carry her through. She was too fast for Ritorubiru to even attempt a backstab. She brought the chainsaw up and across at the big lizard's neck level. With a failed blocking attempt, sparks flew as the cutting edge severed the ancient sword in half; then severed his head from his body in one deft sweep. "Technology destroys tradition," Alice said. "Welcome to the New Industrial Revolution."

She tried to wipe some of the fresh blood from her face that had sprayed all over during the decapitation, "Ugh, smells like gasoline," but she only smeared it more.

"Bravo!" came a voice from behind with a clapping accompaniment. "You are truly a new heroine. Just what this place needs."

The little witch and all the other spectator animals had left except for this one. A weasel.

"Let me guess," Alice said, "Following the habit of obvious nomenclature here, you must be a weasel named Weasel, am I correct?"

"D. Weasel, to be precise, ma'am," he said tipping his bowler hat, "but you can call me Dirty. I would like to offer my services as a cultural tour guide to our wondrous land. I can tell you're not from around here."

Alice pondered his proposal. "Very well, Dirty Weasel, lead the way."

He wrung his paws, "Excellent! Our adventure begins!"

As Alice opened the front gate to leave, the little weasel ran back to the destroyed shed and pulled something from the wreckage. He moved quickly past her and took the lead. He was carrying a baseball bat, "I have a feeling I'm going to need this. It can be a dangerous world but should prove quite the intrepid sojourn indeed!"

"Oops, almost forgot," Weasel said as he went behind a tree to retrieve his hidden belongings. He rigged up a sling to carry the bat, then strapped the silver goggles onto his hat and prepped a small violin, "Gotta have tunes for the trip. Hey diddle diddle gonna play my fiddle," he said, then eased on down the road playing "Turkey in the Straw."

SING A SONG OF CHAINSAWS
A POCKET FULL OF DIE
HAS SHE COME TO SAVE THE WORLD
THIS GIRL FROM OUT OF TIME?

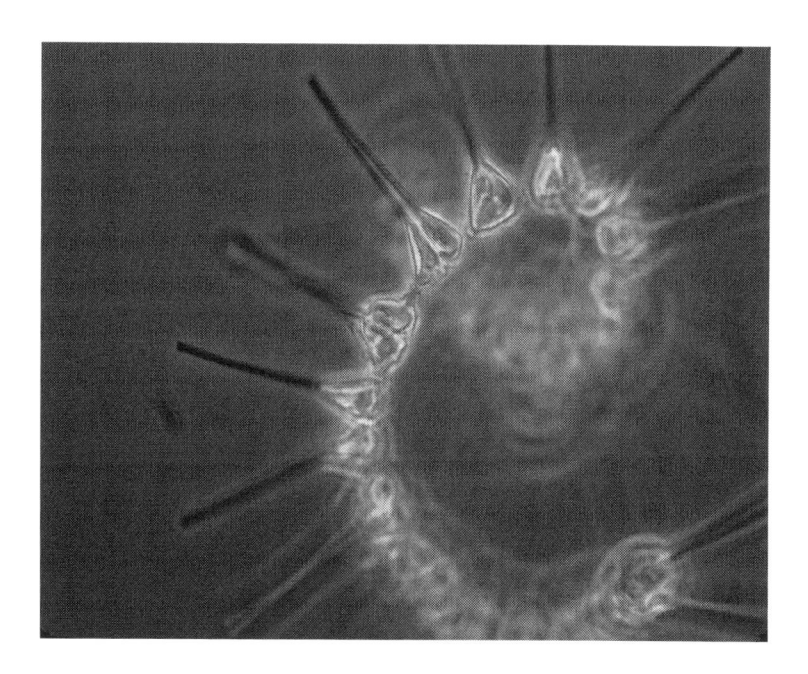

Advice from a Fractapillar - Chapter 9

Time. And space. And shit.

    Alice followed Weasel through the thicketed thoroughfare as he fondly fiddled and frolicked about. She told him all about the interesting people she had met so far this day. The trees began to thin as more and more giant mushrooms appeared until they found themselves walking through a fungi forest.
    Weasel stopped both playing and strolling. Alice had been thinking back on her day and had not noticed until she bumped into him. She saw an enormous wormlike thing. "What is it?"
    "It's a fractapillar," Dirty said. "The larval stage of the vortex butterfly. They fade in and out of the aether, feeding on the mushrooms."
    The creature seemed to vibrate, causing it to solidify more in this reality. It turned and looked at them, "Who aaarrrre yoooooou?" it asked with a voice sounding like the rustling of leaves during an October breeze.

"Just at the moment, I do not know," Alice replied earnestly. "When I got up this morning, I knew somewhat at least, but I have changed several times since then. I think you need to have..."

"What do you mean by that?" the Caterpillar interrupted. "Elucidate."

"I will not be able to explain myself, I'm afraid, because I'm not myself, you see," Alice said.

"You are a person divided. Your aetheric duality is in contrariness. You fight against yourself. You must decide, is the darkness in you, or are you in the darkness. Nature versus nurture. Rapture versus rupture."

"He who fights with monsters should look to it that he himself does not become a monster. And when you gaze long into an abyss the abyss also gazes into you. Friedrich Nietzsche," Alice quoted, then asked of herself, "Who do you see in the looking glass, Alice? A broken little girl? Or a new woman who has pieced herself back together? And what will become of her?"

"I visit this place to harvest mushrooms. Perhaps they can help you as well. They are paradox caps. They help me focus and find myself by expanding my self. Like the cosmic inflation and integration of the universe itself." It began to wiggle about. "If you could step back for a moment."

Alice did as she was asked. It finished ingesting another piece of the mushroom then hovered in the air. "Things change. And so shall I."

She stood transfixed as the fractapillar gyrated and spun a plasma cocoon around itself. Like tiny streaks of lightning solidified, synapses firing, ideas being realized and materialized, creating a living lattice astral womb. It became semitransparent and simply floated in midair, half in this world, half in another.

"A thing of beauty, or of terror, it may become," Alice said, "beauty or terror." She hoisted the chainsaw upon her shoulder. "Weasel!" Alice shouted. "Where have you gotten to?"

"I'm over here!" Weasel replied. He had pulled a small box from his hip bag. He showed Alice a handful of small eggs. He cracked them open one by one and poured the yolks into the box. He closed the lid and flipped a switch and there was a whirring sound from inside. He moved it from paw to paw as it seemed to be getting hot.

Alice gathered some aether silk strands which had fallen away from the cocoon as she walked towards Weasel. They were as pliable as regular silk but were as strong as steel. She was going to make a harness for the chainsaw. "Every cloud has a metal lining," she said to herself.

Weasel pulled two forks out of his bag and handed one to Alice. He popped open the lid to reveal freshly cooked eggs, steam rising from the extraordinary contraption, and said, "Presto! Instant breakfast. It's a Doctor Schwarzen Egger, pat pend, it heats and scrambles eggs at the same time. Handy little device."

Alice couldn't remember the last time she'd eaten, what with time being so wonky here. So they stopped and had a nice little breakfast.

As they made their way to the edge of the mushroom forest they saw quite the sight. A knight mounted on a two-headed sabertooth tiger. He had slimy green tentacles curling out from his back through openings in his armor. He was talking to a robed man with sallow skin and a skeletally thin appearance.

"A Cthulhic knight!" Alice exclaimed. "These rabbit holes are becoming a real problem if this cosmic debris is floating in."

"More otherterrestrial beings?"

"Yes. Including myself, he makes the fourth one today. His companion may be a fifth."

They tried to listen in on the strangers' conversation.

"I only care about getting the zosozo. Then I can return to Herku and take what is rightfully mine," said the boney man.

"You will have your eldritch fuel, enchanter," the knight replied. "Look here! It is all around you! In this world, your precious zosozo grows in a lichenous form. Local workers are being pressed into service as we speak and shall arrive shortly. They will harvest enough for you to take back and lay waste to all the thrones of the OEO."

"This land is unstrung at a dangerous level. I cannot wait to be done with it."

"Cantarugu, why do you think there is such an abundance here? Madness is an energy. It spurs the strength and ardor of the receptive forms."

"You ready, Weasel?" Alice asked.

"Let's do this."

In a literal blur of time energy Alice pushed her pace beyond physical boundaries and blasted towards the cth knight. She leapt in the air and slammed into him like a cannonball. She spun and landed gracefully while he clatter-clanked to the ground. Alice issued a "Yah! Go!" and smacked the saber mount on the rump in an attempt to frighten and spur away the beast, but it had been well trained and refused to be routed. She pulled her chainsaw from its sheath as the knight regained his footing, adjusting the now dented chest plate in amazement at the damage this little girl just did to his armor which was forged in the blood, tears, and forced ejaculate of angelic beings.

Dirty followed as closely behind as he could. He bonked the distracted saber-tooth on both of its heads as he passed and ran toward Cantarugu the pallid mage. Weasel swung on him as soon as he was close enough. Despite his sickly appearance, the enchanter was as strong as a giant and simply reached out and grabbed the bat from the furballer like taking a twig from a child. Never trust a wizard.

So Weasel did a two-paw stomp on the enchanter's foot, wrapped around Cantarugu's leg, held tight, then bit him on the back of the knee. Those sharp weasel teeth found a nice, tender spot and the magic man yelped in pain.

"Ahhh! Scyllaborn, get this animal off of me!" he called out to his tentacular companion. But the cth knight would not be able to help.

Scyllaborn had not taken Alice seriously, considering her success merely an element of ambush. He had thought it amusing to slap Alice on the ass with one of his tentacles--until she chopped it off!

He barely had a chance to draw his sword before Alice had brought the chainsaw down on him. And she was getting better and better with her newfound loveslicer. A little extra turn-and-lift as she connected with his blade allowed her to catch it with the cutting teeth and use the moving chain's velocity to fling the attacking weapon away at high speed. Scyllaborn was barely able to hold onto it.

And with each repulsion of the sword he was left open for

her followup strike of a killsaw thrust to the midsection. Sparks sprayed with each hit as Alice continually grinded away on the Cthulhic knight. His magic armor was not so magical against the skillful attacks from the Lady of the Chain.

Alice stumbled and dropped to one knee as she lunged in again. Scyllaborn went for a strong executing blow, attempting to lop her head off while she was in her vulnerable state. But it was an overstated feint on her part and he fell for it. As he lifted his sword high to get a good downswing, Alice jammed the saw up into his armpit, easily cutting through the inner chainmail mesh as well as most of his arm. It dangled and stretched the remaining shoulder skin with the weight of the armor and sword as blood streamed down his body. Several tentacles held tight to the severed limb as the others struck out at Alice.

In his weakened state she easily began removing the rest of his tentacles with the chainsaw. Blood and slime dripped everywhere.

Cantarugu finally managed to shake the Weasel loose. He grabbed the talisman around his neck and began reciting the magical words to activate its power. Dirty jumped on his back and began choking him with the leather necklace that held the now-glowing item. Weasel clawed at the enchanter's face, but with a brilliant flash he disappeared.

Scyllaborn had crumpled to the ground. Alice kicked him in the chest and forced him onto his back. She stood with one foot on his throat and the tip of the chainsaw blade lightly scraping the face of his helm. "Return to the sublunary harbingers of your dark god, if you dare, and tell them of your opprobrious defeat. This world will not be easily subjugated."

The saber mount remained passive, its owner having been unable to command it during the fight. "Well, at least I got a souvenir," Weasel said holding up the talisman. "I'm sure he'll come looking for it."

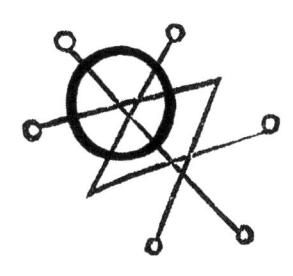

"You move, you die," Alice said as she withdrew the chainsaw and stepped away from the prone cth knight. "Let's go, Dirt."

The duo headed northeast out of the mushroom forest, the area beyond opening into rolling fields. They slowed as they saw a melee unfold before them.

A portly human nearly the size of an ogre had been lying naked on his back in a bed of lush moss. A beautiful faery with long monarch wings had used her magic to grow to the height of a small human and was riding the mammoth masher reverse cowgirl style.

"So, does random killing and fucking happen a lot around here?" Alice asked.

"Yeah, pretty much," Weasel replied.

From the periphery came an onslaught of automapawns, the mechanical infantry of the Red Kingdom. The Red Sergeant was leading them in battle.

"Alright Styge, get your faery fucking fat ass up!" Sarge yelled, "I need answers and you'd better have some, or I'll take them out of your hide!"

Styge stood up, the faery's legs wrapped around him, he held her up with one hand around her waist, and continued to thrust inside her and walk toward the red menace. "I'm busy!" he bellowed. His body became flush as his anger mounted, the muscles tensing and nearly tearing the skin. The faery moaned with the added girth inside her.

"He's a stonewall berserker," Weasel said. "See how he's getting all pumped up and out of control. This should be interesting."

"Should we intervene?"

"Not yet. Let's see what happens."

Jack Fell Down - Chapter 10

> There are three kinds of people--
> Commonplace Men, Remarkable Men, and Lunatics.
> --*Mark Twain*

What is a man? What defines him? Woe, how I have stumbled in every aspect as it is delineated by society. I have failed as a husband. I have failed as a father. I have failed as a man.

Nothing to do, nothing to lose.

Then I wound up here. Leader of a broken army of lost souls. Gambak. The wandering ones. Itinerant mercenaries.

If you can't find a conspiracy to join--start one.

Damn dimensional water gate. When I find that rabbit I'm going to make a furry codpiece out of him. Originally they called me the Well Walker of the Wish Water. Then Wish Walker.

I have just killed the Red King and the White Queen. Their affair discovered, I was attacked, forced to defend myself. If I had softened my blows it would be I counted among the dead instead. Already word has spread and a new title has been bestowed up me--Jack Fell Down, Breaker of Crowns. I am lauded as the people's hero. Empty accolades for the Aristotelian champion. "What good is having all the answers when you cannot implement them?"

Jack wore all black; boots, pants, and a cavalry shirt with an inverted crown freshly painted on the front. He had ripped off the sleeves to allow for better movement during combat. His arm bracer was wound tight with copper wire like a Tesla coil and connected to a control unit in the glove. It generated a small magnetic field that could be used to repel ferrous metals. He wore no metallic items on his person. He carried only a simple wooden sword, for it is the wielder, not the weapon, that is the master.

Dread Penny. Jack's assassin. He was beginning to gain followers, deadly ones. She was dressed from head to toe in formfitting crushed blue velvet except for the stark white balaclava and elbow-length gloves. She wore a porcelain mask with ornate red swirls streaming down from the black eyes. Her fingertips had matching swirls. She wielded a crescent moon sickle. Though she was trim, athletic, and shapely, her hidden visage was inhuman. "I am a *wondrous* horror story. You do not want to know how it ends."

Jack spied the redbots near the perimeter of the mushroom forest. "I'm sure this is about me. Let's go solve the problem." They moved toward the skirmish.

Styge was randomly pumping the faery while he smashed the mechanical footmen. Sarge wielded a baton that he would intermittently thwack the automapawns with and bark orders at them.

"Red leader, command your forces to stand down!" Jack shouted over the battle clatter.

The Sergeant spun around, "Well I'll be bandersnatched, isn't this a nice unbirthday surprise. All units, about face! Kill that trugger! Go! Kill! Kill! Kill!" The automapawns turned and swarmed Jack and his troop.

"Red Fred there might be friend or family to Sultori, I think it's time we stepped in," Alice said. Weasel gave a thumbs up and they joined the fray.

Dread Penny hurled her sickle at Styge. He turned the faery toward the spinning blade and used her body as a shield. The weapon lodged in her breast and pierced her lung. She began coughing up blood. The frenzied fighter pulled the fuck fae off his erect cock and threw her at the masked murderess.

Penny pulled her sickle out of the pixie party girl projectile and with one fluid motion turned and sliced off the flailing faery's head in midair. Both pieces fell to the ground.

Alice leapt atop the stonewall berserker's shoulders and wrapped her legs tight around his head. She cleaned his clock with a quick succession of chronokinetic punches, then casually took a single soft step off the big man as he crashed down.

Since Alice had been engaging the nude nuisance, Penny moved to take out the Red Sergeant. Weasel came in swinging to stop her but she hooked his bat with the sickle then proceeded to kick him once in the stomach and then twice in the head, knocking him for a loop.

Alice yelled, "No!" in a vain attempt to distract Penny. She didn't have enough time, even for someone like her, to pull out the chainsaw and stop the assassin's strike. So she dove into the Sergeant, twisting his arm around and pulling his baton upward, blocking the fatal attack. She slid Sarge to the ground and took the baton.

Dread Penny remained silent and simply stared at the defender.

"Let's dance," Alice said. With a nearly blinding combination of thrusts and parries the two lethal warriors engaged in the precarious exchange. But the baton was getting whittled away.

Alice took three big steps back and was gone! *CRACK!* went Dread Penny's skull as Alice coldcocked her from behind. "Time slip."

Jack's group had easily dispatched the Red regiment. The Sergeant had gotten back up and was ready to engage their entire ragtag army with just his bare fists. Alice pulled out her chainsaw and fired it up as their attentions turned. She moved in front of him. "No more fucking around. People are going to start losing limbs. Red is protected this day. You are done here. One way or another."

Weasel joined Alice at her side.

"Yes. A cessation of conflict is in order," Jack said stepping forward. "But I have a communiqué for the Red Kingdom."

"Endgame," Sarge sneered venomously, which was Chessian for, "I'm going to kill you."

"Let him speak!" Alice snapped. "You are only alive right now because I currently ally with Red. And that is tenuous at best."

A solemn nod expressed Jack's thanks. He addressed the Sergeant, "Your king is dead, at my hands. It was self defense. He would not welcome discretion in our shared matter and sought to silence me permanently. He failed, and paid with his life." The Breaker of Crowns paused momentarily to repose himself, "You may tell your queen, the Gambak are not going anywhere. Her rule does not apply to us. Nor does any monarchy."

"Same game, new players," Alice remarked. "You've said you piece. Now gather your fallen and go your way."

Alice watched and waited until they were gone, night coming on.

She said to the Sergeant, "It is a beautiful red sunset. You are only still here to see it because Dame Desultoria is my friend. Remember that." She walked away from him.

"Should we do something for the faery?" Weasel asked.

"Yes. Let's move her under the cap of that giant blue milk mushroom. I don't know what their methods of decomposition or funeral rites are, so perhaps some of her own kind will find her." She kicked Styge as she walked past, "Wake up, stupid."

STICKY WICKET

Bar Fight at the Open Air Strip Club - Chapter 11

    Alice and Weasel continued down the road apiece until they came upon an outdoor lounge. Various couches and chairs were spread across an immaculate green lawn surrounding long, low cocktail tables, all turned to face a central, raised stage. It was connected to a sunken, brick patio and a narrow bar that stretched across one side of the place. The entire area was surrounded by a high hedge that acted as a privacy fence. The name of the social gathering place, "STICKY WICKET" had been cut rather roughly out of a large metal sign and was illuminated from behind by a large glass tank that was filled with fireflies. It gave off a ghostly green glow in the fading twilight. Wisps of fluffy clouds broke up the waning violet sunset across the rolling horizon just beyond this garden of iniquitous delights.
    "What is this place?" Alice asked.
    "It is a club without a club," Weasel said, adjusting his hat and vest. "One of a more, mature nature. A pleasure garden."
    "Oh, you mean like a gentlemen's club."
    "Haha, yes, but the last way to describe these fellas is gentlemanly." The doorman was the size of a gorilla. Then Alice looked again, it was a gorilla. He blocked Dirty's progress, so the confident weasel simply pushed past, "Look out, ya mooky monkey."
    "Watch yerself, weasel," the gorilla growled.
    "Don't make me beat your ass again," he said looking up at the bruiser, straight in the eye. Weasel had no fear. "This is Sokwe," he said to Alice while never breaking eye contact, "but everyone calls

him Gogo Gorilla, for a multitude of obvious reasons."

"Oh, excuse me, miss. I didn't see you there," Gogo said as he stepped aside and motioned for them to enter.

A female lynx was on the stage dancing for the dozen or so animals in the audience. The only human was a portly gentleman dressed in tailed jacket and formal attire. His bald pate made him appear older than he actually was, but his beard was epic. Alice realized that he was not wearing any pants, only a pair of loose-fitting red and white striped lounge shorts.

"That man is without trousers," she said in astonish.

"Oh! D-man!" Weasel said when he realized who Alice was talking about. "That's Stramash Prang, the Dynamite Man. His family made a fortune with those nitro sticks, which has allotted him the leisure time to pursue his musical passion for concussion percussion, the world's first literal boom band, Detonator Go! He felt the '1812 Overture' was too sedate."

"And, the underwear?"

"He says that his music is so triumphant that his first professional performance actually blew his pants off. He could never go back to wearing them after that."

They joined him and exchanged pleasantries. Stramash leaned back in the comfy padded chair and put his feet up on the quarter barrel that had "TNT" painted in big black letters across it. The matching pony keg beside it had a mechanical pump attached to the top with a hose and spout handle on it.

They all noticed a strange figure appear behind the raised platform as if it had passed without incident right through the hedge wall. It was a man with green skin and leaves growing from his scalp in place of hair. A prehensile vine snaked from his back and over his shoulder. It shot forth and wrapped around the cat dancer's throat, then lifted her into the air.

"Egads!" exclaimed Dynamite Man. "That's Chlorofitus! One of the Six Impossible Things!"

"But what is he doing here?" asked Weasel. "The Six were forbidden by the Queen of Spades from entering these lands. She will not be happy."

Another man pushed his way through the hedge wall and stood beside Chlorofitus. The One-Eyed Jack of Hearts! He was the court's technowizard. He scanned the crowd with his mechanical eye replacement goggle.

"Ah, there is your answer," said Stramash. "The Queen of

Hearts is making her move to usurp the thrones of the other Card Queens."

"Bitches fighting over jewelry. Ain't matriarchy grand," Weasel said sarcastically.

"Oh, it's more than that. Their castle of cards is beset upon from all sides. Chthonic knights everywhere, Wolfco setting up shop, armed disputes along the Chessian Borderlands, the Candians to the south, Gambak mercenaries, Hoppentots, trouble in Trog Town. This does not bode well for any of us."

Jack simply nodded to Chlorofitus. Then another deadly vine sprang from the green man's back. The lynx was hissing and gasping for breath while she clawed at the constricting vine. He drove the sharp edge of the second plant-tentacle up into her anus and dug through her guts.

The catwoman spasmed in pain. He began continually penetrating her with the sex vine, in and out, in and out. With a big thrust, the lynx's skin began to warble beneath her fur, until wicked spikes pierced through the surface of her body. She continued to twitch, but with her innards skewered, she was dead.

With a bucking whip of the violating vine, he ripped her flesh into pieces and flung them off as though he had stuck his fingers in something icky. But the orgasm sap that mixed with her blood and covered the stage, as well as the salacious look upon his face, portrayed his sadistic nature. He passed the vine under his nose and took in her scent; the sickly sweet smell of sex and death.

Jack stepped carefully up on stage. With a wry smile, he announced, "Ladies and gentleman! By decree of the Queen of Hearts, this club is closed!" Unsure if they could safely make it to the exit, and unwilling to turn their backs on these assailants, the club patrons all retreated behind the bar. The few winged creatures easily managed an aerial escape.

Alice just laughed. "Could this be any more fitting? Chainsaw Girl versus the Vegetyrant. Honestly, this is like a bad fantasy novel." She stood up and started the chainsaw. "If you'll excuse me, Mr. Prang, I have a treeman to trim. Weasel, if you would be so kind as to. . ."

"Jack. Yeah, I got him. He's had this beating coming for a long time. Let me finish my drink real quick."

"This should be interesting," said Dynamite Man.

As the others were prepping for battle, Gogo made sure the

customers were safely hidden out of sight. He grabbed a sledge hammer from next to the toolbox under the counter and headed toward the stage.

    Jack saw the Congo strongo approaching. The lenses in his technogoggle began to spin and refocus. He was targeting Gogo. A mechanized arm controlled by the goggle brought a rocket-launching apparatus over Jack's shoulder from a backpack rack and pointed at the approaching primate. Aim and fire! A direct hit!

    Gogo was blasted backwards against the firefly tank. The glass cracked but did not break. He was unconscious.

    In a flash, Alice was across the lawn of the open air strip club and cutting Chlorofitus down to size. A sticky chartreuse sap blood oozed from the severed vines. Another bramble tentacle erupted from his back and swiped at Alice, their pointy thorns almost throbbing in an attempt to pierce her flesh.

    Weasel grabbed an abandoned drink from a table as he sauntered over to the stage. He swigged down the hard cider. Not his favorite, but it was free. He threw the empty glass at the royal card, "I'm coming for you, Jackoff."

    The alcohurled object simply shattered on Jack's red heart-shaped shield. But it would have been for naught regardless. Jack wore heavy armor made from ivory plates with gold joints and accents. But his overconfidence and pretty boy ego would not allow him to wear a helmet, and therein would lie Weasel's triumph and Jack's tragedy.

    "Haha, silly vermin," said Jack, "You wish to engage in melee? Then come and die." He drew a long slender mace from its resting position at his belt. The head consisted of a steel heart bisected by another steel heart.

    Stramash felt around his jacket, "Now where did I put... Ah! here it is." He pulled out a stick of dynamite from his inner pocket. He ran his fingers through his beard and produced a box of matches from its hairy hiding spot.

    He lit the fuse on the stick of dynamite and yelled out, "Alice, my dear! Please take several steps back and the appropriate safety measures." Then he threw the concussive candy cane at Chlorofitus. It landed at the plantman's feet.

    Alice backpedaled and barely made it out of the blast radius. Jack and Weasel were far enough away that they were unaffected.

The dynamite exploded. Shattered strata and sanguiphyll was everywhere.

"Just call him Stumpy! Har har!" guffawed Stramash.

But Chlorofitus the Impossible Thing was not done yet. Alice would change that. Severed plant-tentacles reached out for her as he tried to stand. With precise, even swipes of her chainsaw, Alice cut away all the dangerous foliage and drove her brutal-bladed beauty deep into the chest of the green man and tore his pulpy palpitating heart to pieces.

"Well, that will never do," Jack said as Chlorofitus was felled. The knave had been scuffling with Weasel but neither could gain a foothold against the other. So the smart card shieldbumped Dirty just enough that he lost his balance and fell off the stage. "You slithy sonuva. . ." Weasel said as he fell.

Jack was pressing buttons on a device attached to his belt. The ground began to rumble beneath the entire pleasure garden.

"Oh shit. I think I know who's coming to dinner," Stramash said.

Alice watched the ground and readied her chainsaw but didn't know where to stand.

Weasel was back up on stage and skitterslid under Jack. With a quick upswing of the bat, he broke the device and managed to catch Jack in the codpiece with the same hit. It didn't do any real injury to the royal pain but it was enough to distract him for Dirty to get a good hold on his legs and pull him off his feet due to the gore and slippy sap covering the stage. A swipe of weasel claws across the face infuriated the vainglorious noblesse.

A Bactrian cameloid dancer ran for the exit. Stramash grabbed her as she passed. "Come here, start sucking," he said, whipping his dick out. "Unless you want to end up asshole-inside-out like your kitty cat friend over there lying in bloody furry clumps." Camelgirl blinked a few times, thinking over what he said. She looked over to where her former friend and coworker used to be, then back at him, "Yeah, okay. This better work."

"Oh, it will," he said. "It will." He reached over beside his chair and picked up his dynamite gun. "You know, I really like your kind, with those humps it's like you've got tits everywhere. Yeah, that's it, baby. You work on that gun, I'll work on this one. We'll shoot 'em both off and blow his house down. Hehehe."

The dynamite gun looked like a wide barrel rifle with a large revolving cylinder containing sticks of dynamite. He would cock and release a modified hammer mechanism that functioned like the old fashioned flintlocks and would spark and light the fuse to the dynamite stick inside the chamber. Pulling the trigger released a burst of air from the pressurized tank mounted to the stock. This would launch the stick at its target which would then detonate when its short fuse burned down.

His timing was so impeccable one would think the sticks of dynamite were exploding on impact. He patted the dancer on her scruffy head, "That's it, keep sucking."

He drank straight from the flexible spout of his mechanikeg. He belched and began to recite an ancient incantation.

She kept jerking him off while she looked up and said, "Let me know if you want to put it in."

"Baby, you don't want this magic inside you. It's for our Impossible friends. Keep sucking, almost there. Use lots of spit, I like it slobbery."

She took his whole cock into her mouth and choked herself on it while she licked his balls with her long tongue.

"Oh yeah, you gag hag, take it all," he said. He let her continue her work while he turned his attention to the melee. "Worst things first. I think Jack's had enough stage time." He aimed the dynamite gun at the Jack of Hearts and pulled back the flintspark, "Weasel! Incoming!"

Dirty had been slip-n-slide fighting with Jack when he heard Stramash's command and immediately jumped from the stage, holding his hat so as not to lose it in the descent. Dynamite Man dropped the hammer and let a stick fly. Jack's bright red shield made a perfect target.

The nitrodust boomer hit dead center. The fuse burned down into the wrapper and detonated just as it began to fall. The concussive force knocked Jack back, off the stage. He crumpled as he hit the ground, but had no time to recoup as the blast had shredded and superheated his metal bracer. He rolled around in the grass as he struggled to remove the twisted and searing arm piece. A moment of relief as he finally pulled it free. His shield had flown the opposite direction, but that did not matter as it had been mangled beyond use from the explosion.

"And no encores!" Dynamite Man shouted, then chortled at his own joke.

Jack rubbed his arm then moved to regain his stance.

Weasel would have none of that! Dirty smashed Ol' One Eye right in his technogoggle, shattering the lenses, but the solid brass casing stayed in place. The eye cup quickly filled with blood and then overflowed down his face, streaking his white armor.

"Red really is your color," Dirty said, jumping on Jack's chest and forcing him down on his back. Weasel pummeled him about the head and shoulders with his baseball bat.

"Whoageez!" Weasel exclaimed as he flipfell off of Jack. The hum coming from the tough guy tech toy on the card master's other bracer hinted at what was about to be unleashed. "Energy weapon!" the furry fury yelled as he tumbled away.

Jack fired wildly in an attempt to simply drive away the bat weasel and any other would-be attackers. Pink tinged, burning white hot bolts of electricity crackled and arced through the air. Those who have been struck by Jack's love lightning have said it hurt so good and left them tingling all over. Weasel did not want to find out!

The earth at the front of the stage began to break apart. Tables and chairs overturned. Apparently Weasel's smashing of the device wasn't enough to stop the call. Whatever Jack had summoned up with his gadget was going to be big!

Gogo had come to, woken by the shaking. He ran and leapt in the air, bounced off the stage, then came roaring down on the Jack of Hearts with a two-handed overhead swing of the sledgehammer that broke the love lightning generator and the knave's arm. Jack yelped in pain.

A giant stone hand reached out of the ground and pulled the rest of its body through the breach. An earth elemental, a creature of living rock. It was made of a white limestone, like a mausoleum statue carved from the same quarry as the grave markers surrounding it. But the chest cavity was hollow, with two crude offset windows cut into it.

From out of the upper window flew a Death's Head Black Albatross; ill luck indeed. Its feathers were all pitch black save for the ones across the top of its head and around its eyes which were white and formed the visage of a skull. A haunting site to behold, especially when accompanied by its unearthly squawk; a long, low, eerily humanlike call, like hundreds of dying children calling out for help.

From the lower window came a group of evil fishmen flopping out onto the grass. Spawn of Dagon! The forces of evil within these lands have achieved an infernal alliance. The Queen of Hearts is powerful indeed, but not even she could unite such groups together under her banner, not of her own accord.

"Dammit," Weasel said, looking up at the towering stone being. "Alice, you got those fish fucks? Saw's gonna be no good against this guy."

"I've got them," Alice responded. She stopped gawking at the behemoth and moved to engage the Dagonites.

"D-man! This looks like your specialty!" Weasel yelled.

"Working on it!" Stramash yelled back. "Trust me, he's gonna get BOTH barrels. Bahahaha!"

A shrill keen filled the club. It was the song of the albatross. Everyone began feeling very peculiar. A depressive thickness weighed upon their psyches.

Gogo stepped up beside Dirty. He took a defensive stance in front of the rocking horror, "I've got this 'til Dynamite can finish it. Go take care of that damn bird."

"We'll be eating magic chicken tonight," Weasel said. They both smiled.

"Sounds good. I've got a beerberry basting we can whip up behind the bar."

"Yummy."

The castlesque crusher brought its mighty rock fist down on its two animal adversaries. The primate powerhouse swung his sledgehammer and swatted away the big stoner's hand. Weasel retreated to the sunken brick patio in search of high proof alcohol to bring down the albatross. Though its song did give him a nice buzz. But that wasn't helping his friends in battle.

"Let me ponder," Stramash said to himself. "Ah, yes, Lefkopetra, the Towering Terror. Rarely do the Six Impossible Things appear in one place at the same time, yet alone operate in unison. Strange powers are afoot in these lands. It is a synchronous fortuitousness that we have all converged here this evening to stem the growing tide of malicious entities which seek to drown our fair queendomia. And to think, I shall have killed as many as two Impossible Things before the happiest of hours today."

A sudden look of surprise crossed Stramash's face. "Oh my! Here it comes! Look out, baby!" he said to the camelgagger. She looked up with a confused expression. He kicked her out of the way, just in time.

A magic stream of cum spewed forth from his cock, more so than was humanly possible. A gushing geyser of goo shot into the air. As the jet of jizz splashed down several feet away, instead of pooling on the ground it began to take on a humanoid shape. Dynamite Man had summoned his own elemental to fight the Impossible Thing, a cum elemental!

The semenman sloshed toward the moving monolith that was still engaging the primate protagonist. It was not quite as tall or as strong as Lefkopetra but would be able to keep the transient tower busy while the rest of them figured out how to destroy it.

Splashfist after splashfist pounded the rock lifeformation. Gogo was not thrilled about the residual splatter that he was being covered with, but he continued to fight on.

Alice made quick sushi of the Dagonites.

Weasel had found a bottle of Blackcardi highfire rum. It was flammable. He took a big swig of alcohol and held it in his mouth. He obtained a mechaspark lighter from the bartender. As the albatross circled the open air club Weasel would spit fire at it. His fur got singed a scintilla when the angry avian buffeted him with its great wings. The wind it generated blew the fireball back at him.

Alice sat her chainsaw down on a cocktail table and jumped on top of the bar at its far end. "Weasel, wait for it to pass over again. When it is between the two of us, then blow the flames. I'll try and get it from behind."

Weasel did as planned. In a brilliant display of speed and agility, Alice raced along the bar and leapt into the air at the low flying albatross. She managed to grab a handful of tail feathers but the bird slipped from her grasp. In its split attention between fire and grabber, the disconcerted albatross simply flapped and hovered in place.

Alice bounced to the back bar counter and climbed the mirrored shelves like a ladder; bottles, glasses, and decorative knick-knacks went everywhere. It gave her enough extra altitude to make another attempt at the fearsome fowl. She jumped over and landed atop the albatross!

Unable to maintain its position with the extra weight and from being knocked off balance, the two came crashing down on the patio. The ebon avian had landed hard. It could barely move. Out of necessity and pity, Alice glommed its head and snapped its neck.

Weasel felt a tinge of sympathy for the majestic creature, but it passed at the thought of the damn good eatz they were going to have tonight; if they lived through it.

"Gogo!" Stramash yelled, "Look out!"

The primate punisher removed himself from the fray. "At least he didn't make another cum joke," he thought.

Another litwicked stick of dynamite went whooshing by. A perfect shot landed it in the chest cavity of the man-mountain. KA-THWACK-BOOM! "What a magnificent echoing sound!" Dynamite Man said of the sound the blast made. "I will have to incorporate the destruction of living rock into my next concert."

The partially contained explosion kept most of the kinetic energy within it body, causing tremendous damage to its rock structure. Fissures formed across its right arm and torso. The cum elemental flowed like a living wave and filled up the hard rocker's insides. It began beating at the weakened spot. Gogo moved back into position and smashed the stoner's right arm, shattering it to pieces.

Lefkopetra reached inside itself and squeezed the jizzemental, pressing D-man's seed soldier against the internal back wall of its body cavity until the wad wave burst, unable to maintain its contained humanoid shape, and waterfalled out the bottom orifice of the rocky horror.

Gogo began hammering away at boulder boy's feet. Lefkopetra looked down at him. A radiant beam of light issued forth from its eyes. The gorilla goombah was both burned and blinded.

Alice strode confidently toward the terrible tor. "Hold your fire, Stramash," she said. The brave new girl stood in front of Gogo, shielding him from any further attacks. Lefkopetra raised its remaining arm and slammed it down on Alice. She put her hands up and unleashed her chronokinetic power, "Even mountains shall crumble in time." The Towering Terror broke into a million pebbles that then turned to dust and gently wafted down around her. "Nothing's impossible."

Weasel sauntered up to her, "Excellent work, my dear. Though it looks like Jack 'strategically retreated' during the battle. I'm sure we'll be seeing him again soon enough. We'll go over all the political machinations, some of them quite literal, of our wondrous land. Tonight, we celebrate!"

"Thank you, Weasel." She wiped her face on her pinafore. "Do they have any facilities here, where I can clean up? I really need to remember to wear my goggles next time. This whole reality is very messy."

"Yeah, let me check with Gogo." Weasel called out, "Hey, Gogo! You guys still got that shower in back hooked up to the mechanical pump from the brook?"

"Yeah," he looked over at Dynamite Man, "I think we could all use a good washing. I'll get some towels."

"Haha! My dick helped!" Stramash cachinnated. "Googoo, I mean, Gogo, you've got white on you."

"I really hate this job sometimes," Gogo said to himself as he went to find the towels.

"When, the fuck, did you learn to do that?" Weasel asked Stramash. "And why didn't you tell me about it?"

"Well, being in the make-things-go-boom business, it became beneficial to learn a smidgen of hydromancy. My own elemental fire department."

"Ah, an ounce of prevention indeed."

"Turns out, you can summon water elementals through whatever liquid you have on hand as a portal from their world to ours. And they take on the properties of the summoning fluid. Thus, the cum elemental."

"Why not a beer elemental, then?"

"And risk wasting all that beer? Plus, why pass up the opportunity for a free blowjob?"

"Points taken."

They had a wonderful feast of beerberry basted albatross and dandelion wine. Everyone retired for the evening and left for their respective abodes. The weather was nice so Weasel and Alice slept out on the big lawn.

The Yellow King - Chapter 12

After a breakfast of beer and stale pretzels the two started out again upon their adventure. An overgrown path of yellow bricks, many broken and displaced by the viny verdure, which in its odd growth seemed more to be keeping something in rather than keeping something out, lead into a wabing boscage.
"Where does that path lead?" Alice asked.
"The Yellow Kingdom. But no one calls it that. Normally they refer to it as the Fallen Kingdom, or the Kingdom of Lost Hope. Actually its more like the Kingdom of Lost Minds, but what passes for sanity around here is debatable to begin with," Weasel said. "The Yellow King and a few of his sad pawns which still serve him are all that remain there. He has no queen, no knights. His bishops are dundering momeraths."
"What are momeraths?"
"It is an expression which literally means foolish counselor. It was they who brought about the fall of the Yellow Kingdom."
"How so?"
"Well, the Chess Kingdoms, as you know, distinguish their individual commonwealths by color, and have been warring amongst themselves for years. The Card Kingdoms have for the most part left them to their own squabbling devices, believing them too small to

pose any real threats to the Houses of Cards.

"So the yellow bishops sought to steal the magical power of a long dead ruler, the Black King. Today, as we know the various realms, there is no Black Kingdom. Some say it is just a myth, or a parable to teach future generations. Others say the White King destroyed everyone and everything in the Black Kingdom. And in its absence the other Chess Kingdoms arose.

"But steal someone's power they did. The Yellow King wielded a preserved human heart that was said to still beat when its dark powers were called upon. It had been preserved for 99 years in a cask of cognac. It is said that the horrors it unleashed were unspeakable, and they tore the Chess Kingdoms apart.

"That is when the Black Knight appeared, his helmet in the shape of a raven's head instead of the traditional horse. He uttered but a single sentence, "You are undone." Then all the horrors dissipated like shadows at sunrise and the Black Knight proceeded to kill almost everyone in the Yellow Court. Besides the King and the Bishops, I am told that the Yellow Trull fled to safety."

"I have to go there."

"What? Nobody goes there. It's crumbling ruins."

"I have to go there. You don't understand, there is a pull in that direction. It's part of being a chrononaut. I'll explain later. Follow me. We have to take care of a lesser evil."

Weasel just shook his head and readied his bat.

They soon came to a dilapidated castle made from the same yellow bricks as the road. There was no defensive wall. It was as if the greenery was trying to swallow the fallen fortress.

In the outer courtyard before the open portcullis was a deteriorating portable puppet stage in red and yellow stripes. Two men wearing priestly robes and tunics each operated a marionette.

One marionette was garbed in royal dress and wore a crown, the other was a strange sea creature, something akin to a mermaid but much more imposing; the top half was a naked woman and the bottom half was twisted tentacles.

Both men wore pale, faceless metal masks that gave them a ghostly appearance. The faceplates were scratched and rusted. How they could see was a mystery. Perhaps the masks were meant for punishment as opposed to intimidation.

One mask had the word "ROBBER" imprinted across the forehead, with the two B's facing each other and turned at a 90 degree angle, as if to give the appearance of gnashing teeth.

The other mask had "Y?" scraped into the metal as if with a heavy tool, or claw.

They were reciting lines from their bizarre puppet play, but their words were muffled. Apparently "April's lost love" was the touchstone of the diminutive drama; whether in reference to a person, or the month, or perhaps the foolish spirit of young love was uncertain.

Alice paused briefly to try and decipher any meaning from their piteous performance.

"High priests laid low. Let us leave them to their madness," Weasel said.

"Yes. It is best," she replied. "Let them still think themselves gods of their world, no matter how small or insignificant."

To either side of the portcullis was a lion statue, sitting, with one forepaw extended, carved from the same stone as the road and castle. There were three roosters washing the lions. The chicken champions each wore a brass shaffron decorated with a small rondel and center spike, as well as a brass scalemail shirt covered in a drab yellow tunic. With their jerky, clunky, clucky motions they looked like windup clockwork unicorns. Hah! What a sight! Keeping the lions polished and spotless gave them the illusion that their kingdom had not fallen down around them. Seeing the uninvited visitors, the three cocks blocked their ingress.

"The paltry, poultry pawns of the Yellow King," Weasel said. "I'm getting kind of hungry. You chickens disease free? I just might gobble you up!"

"What next? Are you going to pull out a fork and knife and chase them around the courtyard?" Alice asked, suppressing a giggle.

"I just might. I just might."

"We are no mere pawns. We are the Royal Guard in Yellow!" clucked loudly a bravehearted banty.

"I am no chicken!" another squawked in reference to his courage and not his kind.

The third was trying to think of something poignant to say but could not come up with anything.

"Alright you little peckers, enough of this," Alice said as she pulled out her chainsaw and started it up. The birdbrains scattered, abandoning their post. The puppeteering priests did not even acknowledge the sound and their play continued undaunted. Perhaps to them it was just the roar of a distant dragon. They should pray they give Alice no reason to bite them. Her teeth are deathly sharp.

The time striker and her furry companion entered through the portcullis and into the grand foyer. They checked some of the rooms in the side hallways but then returned to the main area which lead to what must be the throne room at the end of the high-ceilinged foyer. Alice pulled open the double doors and walked in.

There upon his brick throne sat the Yellow King. He was dressed in yellow, rotting, royal robes. His skin was a similar sickly color. His great red wings were folded at his shoulders. There was an energy corona encircling his head. Various weapons and empty suits of armor were scattered about. A fallow dust covered everything.

Kneeling before him was the actual tentacled sea-she corresponding to the effigial puppet. But she was paying homage to another crown. For the king's robes were open and she was performing oral sex on him. But he had five dicks!

They were in a circular pattern with one penis at each point of a pentacle. Alice had heard about ancient star stones but she was pretty sure that it was in reference to actual highly sought after enchanted artifacts as opposed to just a vague sexual euphemism used as a sick joke by cosmic beings to get blowjobs.

She was sucking the top one. The next two below that she was jerking off, one in each hand. The bottom two she was using her tentacles to jerk them off. She turned and made a gurgling hiss at the intruders. They were unsure if the gurgling was due to her fishy nature or the star stone ceremony had already lit the first of five fleshy candles.

The octopussy stopped what she was doing and began crawling toward the side of the throne where a makeshift well had been made from a large assembled pile of the yellow bricks. Her strong tentacles lifted her the rest of the way up and over the edge with a splashing exit.

"Dammit. That's why we're here," said Alice. "The well is a dimensional portal."

"You had best be an emissary from one of the other Chess Kings sent to negotiate peace talks, and to take the place of that last one."

"You'll be lucky if we don't snap your spine and make you skullfuck yourself, all holes filled," Weasel said. Alice just sneered in gleeful agreement.

"You should know," Alice said, "that if I have the capacity to track down rabbit holes, even haphazardly opened and maintained ones such as yours, then I am more than able to destroy said gateway and anyone who stands in my way in doing so. Obviously, you are not a native Chessian, but you are trapped here for whatever ills you have done. But that matters not to me. Will you yield?"

The red halo around the king's head glowed brighter. Alice experienced a strange surge inside her mind, but shook it off. Weasel was not so lucky. He dropped to the ground holding his head in pain.

"Alice. Can't, control, my thoughts. Horrible visions. Things, inside, my head," Weasel stuttered out as he rolled around on the floor.

Alice was pissed.

With lightning speed she flanked the throne and retrieved several bricks from the pile next to the well. Grab, turn, throw, throw, throw. Three direct hits to the king's head. His energy crown dimmed and flickered as he slumped, stunned.

"I don't have time for this," Alice said. She stormed up to the Yellow King and pulled him off the throne by his tattered robe. She used the momentum to catapult the semiconscious monarch into the well. The scarf covering his inhuman face fell away as he yelled out, "No!" Alice smashed the king on the head with another brick then pushed him underwater as far as she could reach without falling in herself.

She grabbed a mace that was part of a pile of armor and began knocking loose the poorly constructed well. Water spilled over onto the floor.

"Here, use this. It will be much faster." Weasel had come up behind her, one eye still squinting in pain. "A gift from our friend, D-man." He handed her a stick of dynamite and the lighter from the strip club.

Alice sat the boombringer on the lip of the well and kept it in place with a brick. She pulled a penny from her pocket and dropped it in. "I wish these cosmic sea gods would fuck off." She lit the fuse and they ran out of the throne room. Big bada boom!

"Hopefully that fucking king was just coming back up as the dynamite went off," said Weasel.

"You got any more of those?" Alice asked.

"Yeah. Four more. And hey, why didn't the king's mind attack work on you?"

"Time is an energy. It is held to the same laws as the rest of the universe, just most people can't effect it. Time can effect madness, but madness cannot effect time. So I'm pretty much immune. You know the expression, 'Where is your mind?' Chrononauts cannot answer that question."

"How about, 'When is your mind?" Weasel joked.

"That one's even worse," Alice laughed. "Darn it, and the king had such nice boots. I had planned to take them from him but I was caught up in the moment and completely forgot."

"Well, there is a cobbler nearby if you are in such a way that you desperately need new footwear."

"Yes, yes I do. This cobbler wouldn't happen to live in a hollow tree and bake cookies by any chance?"

"No. But he does have a moonshine still out back."

"Excellent! We shall go there!"
"Then let's ransack this place and see what we can salvage that might be of any value!"
"Yes, let's!"

These Boots Were Made for Kicking Your Ass - Chapter 12, Subsec A

On the way to the cobbler's they saw a new poster plastered over an old Wolfco one. It had a picture of a businessman with a bare skull instead of a regular head with the words "DEATH MANAGER FUCK OFF!" painted across the jacket.

Alice traded some of the golden knick-knacks that they had scavenged from the Yellow King's castle for a nice pair of combat boots. Stompy Fun Time ahead!

"How do they fit?" Weasel asked.

"Pretty good," Alice said. "We'll have to see how they do in combat." And as an afterthought, "And I still need to find someone who can fix rusted hearts. I asked the cobbler but he said he couldn't help."

"I guess the old adage of 'only time' doesn't apply to mechanical parts, huh."

"Hey! Gimme back my lighter!"

A Black Rainbow on Babbage's Birthday - Chapter 12.6

"That is a peculiar looking creature. What is it?" Alice asked the elderly gopher of her canvaswork.
"I do not know," she replied, moving rhythmically back and forth in her rocking chair. "It's called psychic needlepoint. I simply relax, close my eyes, and the universe speaks to me. I guess you could say it tells me what I need-le to know! Haha!" she slapped her knee at the joke she had made.
"Hello, Granny G," Weasel said as he came up beside the two ladies. "How you doin'?" he asked as he gave her a big hug.
"Oh fine fine," she answered. "The weather's been right nice. Mild breeze blowin' through the salix trees, and I've just been here sittin' in the sun and embroiderin' away. Been a might inspired as of late. A real pleasure workin' with that fancymancy boy." She picked up the crooked little wooden frame again, closed her eyes, and began to hum as she started back in with the needle and thread and continued rocking to and fro.

"It's infomancy, dear heart," came a voice from a short distance away beneath the shade trees. "Would you like anymore lemonade, Granny?"

"No thank you, Thomas."

"And would our visitors like any?"

"Yes, that would be most delightful," Alice said as she moved toward the spot where the voice came from. A teenage boy, the aforementioned Thomas, was sitting at a wooden stand with a large glass punch bowl, several pitchers, and drinking glasses sitting atop it. A sign attached to the front read "FREE LEMONADE and INFO CO-OP." Erected behind the stand was a large difference engine; a machine used for storing, retrieving, and processing information.

"What is an info co-op?" Alice asked as Thomas poured her a glass of lemonade.

"Information cooperative. I am creating a directory of knowledge that can be referenced freely by anyone, but first I must gather as much data as possible. That is what I do. I am an infomancer. I'm Thomas, if I may formally introduce myself by the way. Good to make your acquaintance."

"I am Alice, pleased to meet you," she said, tipping her head in acknowledgement as she took another drink. "I assume the free lemonade is an enticement to get passersby to stop and chat."

"Exactly. Got any useful information you'd like to donate?"

"Well, I assume you've already been told about the transdimensional rabbit holes they have around here."

"Yes, this place is a strange, unstable nexus for them. That's how I came to be here myself."

"You followed the White Rabbit down here, too?"

"No, though I've met multiple 'travelers' that have told me of this rabbit's tricks. But apparently singing along to incantations on audio cassettes is just as effective as reading it aloud yourself from some ancient magical text."

"You mean sound recordings? What year are you from?"

"Yes, apparently there was more to the middling punk band Richard Hell and the Voidoids than the projection of their teen angst and general malaise would have us believe. I'm from 1985. But none of our past timelines were anything even remotely like this."

"Yeah, they've got some pretty freaky shit going on. What were you saying about the instability of the portals?"

"After gathering about a dozen locations of different rabbit holes, I went on a field excursion and visited each one. All of them are in varying stages of fluctuation. Some are perfectly fine, others are having trouble maintaining their solidity or dimensional integrity, and some have already collapsed. Whoever is opening them all is not very good at it."

"It's a time trap. They're luring various beings into this reality for some nefarious reason and it's going to get this place torn apart." Alice finished her lemonade. "If I find out anything else about what's going on I'll try to get word back to you. Knowledge is power."

"Agreed. Would like anymore lemonade?"

"No, thank you. Is that embroidery of Granny's an aether bug that has been emerging as a consequence of the rabbit hole fluctuation?"

"I believe so. I have not encountered any myself. All my information so far has come from her precognitive sewing ability. I've been calling them Aquarii since one of her needleworks had another figure pictured with the symbol and the backdrop was the Aquarius constellation. Whatever is coming through and agitating the time-space field is a contemporary to Cthulhu, who was just a fictitious mythological figure to me in my mundane world until a few weeks ago. An encounter with a few of His spawn and some Dagonites convinced me of his very real nature, at least here."

"Yes. I'm still getting used to the whole talking animals thing."

"Still weirded out, huh," Weasel said chuckling as he walked up and grabbed a glass of lemonade. "I guess I would be, too. How's the info biz, Thomas?"

"Slow-going, Dirt, but it's getting there. Anything new underground? Anything shakin' in Weasel City?"

"Nah. Same ol', same ol'."

"Oh, I've got a question for you!" Alice proclaimed. She pulled the painted chess piece from her pocket and showed it to Thomas.

"I know this one without even looking it up," he replied. "Though it is obviously a queen chess piece, this stylized design on the side is for the Blue Basilisk, a faery Chessian. There are multiple accounts describing it as a reptile, or a fowl, or varying degrees of both. Regardless, she does possess the same death gaze as the beast of legend. She sends these to her would be victims. She holds no official title, there is currently no Blue Queen. She is addressed as Lady Basila, and to do so otherwise incites her wrath."

Suddenly, there was a rattle-rumbling coming from down the dirt road. A shiny, bright red open-air steam car was flinging dust everywhere and barreling down on them. The outline of a heart had been painted on the hood and doors in white. The toad driving the hot rod yelled out, "I am the newly ordained Honorary Knave of Hearts! Feel my wrath!" Sitting in the passenger seat next to him was the White Rabbit.

"Speak of the furry little devil and he shall appear," Alice said.

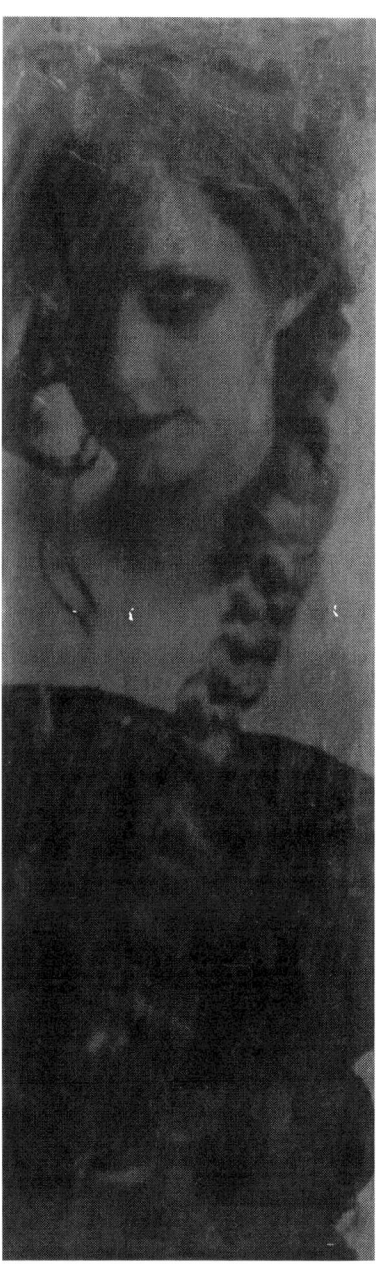

A woman stood up in the backseat and removed her white hooded cloak. Her fringed red bob flowed with the wind. She was completely naked except for her white boots and the huge mechanical gauntlets. Her pubic area was shaved clean but bore a large spider tattoo across her vagina, the upper legs running up her stomach, the lower legs running down her inner thighs. A red heart was tattooed on her right arm, with another one above it inverted. She was the Two of Hearts.

"Hold it steady, Toad."

"Yes, Tuella. I am your faithful, motorized charioteer."

A solid, Renaissance-figured woman, Tuella was a fighter and had the scars to prove it. Her weighty weapons of ass(kickery) destruction looked like the Jack's handiwork. Since he couldn't get the job done, a professional was sent out in his place.

And that rabbit has a way of finding people.

As the car whizzed past, the Two leapt from the backseat and tried to land atop Alice, raising a massive mechafist as she flew through the air. She brought it down with a precision strike, trying to pound Alice into the ground. But the clock rocker was too fast for that.

It was difficult for Alice to stand from the seismic shockwave. She equalized herself then pulled out the chainsaw and made it sing!

Alice rushed at Tuella with a series of short, quick, back and forth swipes. Sparks flew as the deadly deuce blocked the attacks with her metal mitts. She even momentarily caught the spinning blade and moved in with a sweeping kick to knock Alice off her feet.

Alice jumped and spun backwards, pulling the saw blade free, then returned with a round of thrust and parry.

For whatever reason there was lots of bad blood between toads and weasels. Dirty couldn't wait to have at the mototoad. As the steam car slowed and turned around, the wily weasel jumped on the driver's side running board and began batting the vehicle's occupants, thumping them several times each.

Whitey reached into the glovebox and pulled out a hand grenade covered in metal hearts. He was so flustered and inexperienced in combat that he tried to throw the grenade at Weasel.

"What are you doing?!?!" Toad shouted.

Weasel ducked the projectile which detonated in the woods beside them. Thomas was hurrying Granny G to safety. Seeing his friends in danger made the manic mustela irate. "Gonna make rabbit stew tonight!" He leaped into the backseat and continued swinging at the duo.

Rabbit pulled out another grenade. "No! Stop it!" Toad yelled at him, but Rabbit ignored the Wetlander's cries and threw the explosive at Weasel. He knocked it down with his bat. It landed on the floorboard beneath him.

"Go boom, bye bye!" Weasel said as he jumped from the moving motorcar. He landed well enough in the soft grass and tumbled away, scampering to get out of the blast radius.

Toad and Rabbit both abandoned the vehicle. "Ooooooh, not again!" Toad bemoaned. The grenade exploded then caused a secondary detonation to the pressurized steam chamber, scalding water sprinkling everywhere.

The flaming wreckage still managed to careen forward out of control. "Idiots," Tuella said as she stepped back and away from Alice, letting the burning buggy pass between them. She reached down and used her manufactured muscle to flip the car over at Alice.

The chopper champ managed to step in pace away from the ambulant automobile, but the twisted rear bumper caught her shoulder. It ripped her sleeve and burned her badly, the top layer of skin instantly baked onto the hot metal and pulled from her body. There was a sickly sweet smell from the singed flesh.

Alice's entire arm was throbbing with pain, making it hard to lift the chainsaw. Two closed in with a wicked grin on her face and began swinging her massive meatmashers.

Alice dropped the chainsaw, knowing she would not be able to properly wield it to defend herself. The furious fister continued her ferrous flurry. It was easy enough for Alice to dodge and withdraw, but with only one arm fully functioning she couldn't mount a direct assault.

Weasel came up behind Toad and knocked him out cold with the baseball bat. He then turned and chased the fleeing Rabbit into the woods.

Tuella pressed her advantage and continued advancing on Alice. The timefighter would have to use her wits to defeat the Deuce.

Alice concentrated and set a concordance with Tuella's attack rhythms. She began using her good hand to tap away the flying mechafists, using the momentum of the swings to slightly, slightly, continually redirect the Two's brutal automatouch. Until she was off-balance enough and BAM! a chronocrusher straight jab right to the snot locker.

Blood gushed from Tuella's nose and down her neck and breasts. "Red is my favorite color. How did you know? Thanks for the fashion tip."

Alice tagged her again.

The sound of her cheek bone breaking could be readily heard and her face began swelling. "Keep talking," Alice said. Move and strike. Move and strike. Move and strike. Alice was pummeling the heart hammer into submission, one-handed!

Dazed and confused, the Two backed away. She raised and held her knee. Tuella flexed her pelvis and blew a spray of hundreds of living spiders out of her vagina!

The creepy crawlies covered Alice and their venomous effects were already beginning to take hold from the multitude of bites. The neurotoxicity was causing a rigidity in her muscles and she felt nauseous. She had to strain to hold down the bile building in the back of her throat.

With a twist of time, Alice shifted her body partially out of sync with reality. The arachnids could not maintain their grip upon her and fell to the ground in an undulating pile. Tuella tried to continue the fight but Alice's presence was obfuscated by the blurring effects of her chronokinetic power and she could not get a good swing on her spiderspun adversary.

Now having the upper hand, Alice was able to land several more punches.

As a last ditch effort to cover her retreat, Tuella began spraying bursts of sticky silk from her clitoral spinneret in a random manner. Though some of the webbing did attach to Alice revealing her position, it was not enough to slow her down. Tuella chose to withdraw from the combat.

Alice let the Deuce go, dropped to her knees, and vomited.

Thomas returned from moving Granny Gopher to safety. He began stomping on and scattering the pile of spiders. "Black widows. Multiple bites. Third degree burn. Be right back."

He made a mud compress for her shoulder and presented a small vial labeled "SLAKE OIL"

"What is slake oil?" Alice asked.

"It gives you what you need," he replied. "It will function like an antivenom in this case. This place has such wondrous things."

She drank it and a majority of the pain and stiffness subsided. "Thank you. Give me a moment to collect myself so I can kick in my accelerated regenerative ability."

"You have healing hands?"

"No, that's usually bleeding hearts and stigmatics, other holy roller types. I'm a chrononaut. I can greatly increase the rate of my natural healing process."

"Oh, time jumper type, huh."

"There's a little more to it than that, but yeah, basically."

"No wonder you were so interested in the rabbit holes."

"While I think about it, could you check your data contrivance for any machinist, or technomage, or other such specialist. I've got a friend with a rusting mechanical heart. If it doesn't get fixed soon she will die."

"Let me check." Thomas went to the difference engine and began typing and pulling levers with a determined celerity.

Weasel came back from his rabbit hunt empty-handed. "Little sucker is fast."

"Don't worry about it," Alice said. "We'll catch up to him eventually. I'm sure he'll be at the queen's *brilliant* soiree," she ended with a high air of sarcasm.

Thomas returned, "Sorry Alice, no dice."

She looked at him puzzlingly.

He laughed, "Oh, that's 1985 slang. I don't have any listings for those professionals you were enquiring about. But I've only just started gathering information."

"That's alright, I'll find someone. It's just a matter of looking."

"For Patina?" Weasel asked.

"Yes," Alice replied.

"How's Granny, Thomas?" Weasel looked toward the infomancer.

"She's fine. More irritated that her knitting was disturbed than the actual fact that she could have been injured."

"Haha, that sounds like her. Glad she's okay."

"I've got something that might help in your gathering of knowledge," Alice said to Thomas, "or you can at least trade it or give it to someone who will find it useful." She pulled out a piece of folded parchment. "It's a looking glass map. Instead of showing where you *can* go, it shows were you *will* go."

"Wow," Thomas said, taking the map, "I heard about these. Thank you! It shows the best course of action when you concentrate on a specific question. Plausibility plus practicality equals potentiality. Like a, not a magic 8 ball, what would you guys call it, um, an oracle board."

"Oh, is that how it works? Still does me no good," Alice said. "I already knew we were going castle crashing."

Thomas had a curious look on his face. "It smells like, Christmas 1978."

"Really?" Alice chuckled. "What does the future smell like?"

"Pretty good. Pretty damn good."

"Thankfully."

"Granny Gopher might be able to use this in conjunction with her stitchwork. Thanks again! And good luck on your quest!" he said as he went to play with his new psychic toy.

"Where's Toad at?" Weasel wondered aloud. "I coldcocked him and left him in the middle of the road."

"He must have come to and wandered off when we weren't looking. I'm still feeling it, but I'm ready to travel," Alice said.

"You sure?" Weasel asked.

"Yeah. I'll be good as new lickety-split."
"I understand the reasoning behind it, I get it, because we're the god damn heroes, and it's the right thing to do, but why are you trying so hard to help a girl that you only met lasterday hereabouts?"

Alice hesitated to answer.

"Because I know what it's like when someone else controls your heart."

Pig and Pepper - Chapter 13ish

    Alice crouched, hidden at the edge of the woods, looking at the house for several minutes. Weasel had just caught up with her. He continually lagged behind because he kept poking his head into the bushes, searching for who-knows-what. She motioned for him to be silent, then waved him forward to join her.
    There were two of the fishmen like they had fought the night before, standing guard at the door to a small cottage. A scarecrow had been hung from a noose at the edge of the front porch overhang, probably used for combat training. One was absentmindedly swinging the human effigy back and forth while the other stared off into the distance.
    In their evolutionary process they had gained humanoid form, retaining their fish head and bulbous eyes while losing their

tails, or they were shrunken and regressed, tucked into their pants. These two wore a royal-looking garb that Alice did not recognize. They were each armed with a pike; the polearm weapon, not the fish. That would be silly, a fishman wielding a fish like a spear. A curious feeling very.

"Ah, more Dagon warders," Weasel said. "They are the spawn of one of the many dark fish gods who rule the deep, sunless oceans. Did you know, there are multiple oceans stacked upon oceans which connect to subterranean worlds. Some say, it even flows into a cosmic sea called the Deep Blue. Not very original, but they're fish, so whatcha gonna do."

I've heard tell of such a place. They called it the Midnight Sea. From the *Tale of the Holy Diver*. Let's get to work," Alice said, this time remembering to lower her goggles before going into battle. "You might want to put yours on, too," she remarked to Weasel, "there's going to be a lot of blood."

"You know, it isn't etiquette to cut anyone you've been introduced to, "Weasel said. "I read that somewhere."

She stepped out of the woods, addressed the fishmen, "Pleased to meet you," and started up the chainsaw, "My name is Alice." She turned to Weasel and said, "Fuck propriety," then charged at the two warders.

"Fish fillet for lunch. Yum." Weasel rubbed his belly, raised his bat, and followed Alice into the fight.

They made a gurgling garbled groaning sound and raised their pikes. Alice stopped short, whipped the saw in a downward arc, then brought it back, chopping through the elongated spear tips in the upswing.

Dirty flanked wide and began beating on the spawn of Dagon. One in the knee then one in the head. Pop! Pop! goes the weasel.

With a thrust of the chainsaw, Alice gutted the other fishman. "Look out, Weasel!" she shouted.

He stepped back and gave her room. She lopped off the fish head of the remaining warder and it went roly polying across the lawn. Blood splattered all over Weasel.

"Awww, fishy fur. I need to wash this off NOW before it dries." He stopped preening and bent down to pick up an envelope that was sitting on the doorstep. He opened it, "An invitation to play croquet with the queen. The envelope is addressed to the Duchess, but the invitation is blank. Here ya go." He handed the invitation to

Alice.

She lifted her goggles. "Hmm. The Queen of Hearts cordially mandatorially invites you and a guest to play croquet tomorrow afternoon, aftertea, in the Royal Rose Garden. Looks like we're going to a party. But there's no time listed."

"Yes it does," Weasel said, "says right on it, aftertea. Aftertea is short for afternoon tea, which is at 4 o'clock."

An earsplitting shriek filled the air. Emerging from the edge of the forest was a Dagon spawned abomination. It was an orca humanoid that stood nearly twenty feet high. A horned ridge surrounded its terribly toothy maw. A similar row of spiked plates ran down the length of its back, growing smaller as they crested the tail. Bipedal, it moved in a semi-upright gait similar to a gorilla. While the coloration was similar to that of an orca it appeared more like an extinct prehistoric beast.

The monstrosity charged across the grassplot directly at Alice! She raised and revved her saw, ready for the attack. It was almost on top of her when Weasel pulled the scarecrow free from the noose and tossed the rag bag body at the bounding behemoth. The creature stopped in mid-run, tearing up turf as it braked, and caught the pumpkin patch protector in its gaping jaws and shook it violently. Then it rolled over on its side and kept throwing the scarecrow up in the air to itself? It was playing catch!

Weasel could see the confused look on Alice's face. "Know your enemy," he said. "There's a reason we call them dag dogs." He laughed, then rubbed the beast's big belly.

"Though it looks fearsome, that is not its nature," she said.

"We lucked out with the saber-tooth earlier. This one, it and I have met before. They were abusive to it, which you would expect from evil fish people. But they made the mistake of letting it wander. Gave it a brickle bar, friends for life."

There was a terrible racket going on inside the house. So much so that they apparently hadn't heard the roaring chainsaw or the gurgling goodbyes of the fish folk. The sound of kettles and dishes being smashed to pieces, big crashes and sometimes sneezes, was going on in a most extraordinary noise. "There's no sense in knocking," Alice said as she opened the front door.

To the right, an entryway led to a large kitchen which was full of smoke from one end to the other. There was a baby in a cauldron atop the counter. The Duchess was sitting on a three-legged chair in the middle of the room. And a cook was reclining against the fireplace, stirring a large soup pot over the flames.

There was a cloud of pepper as the cook flavored the soup beyond good taste, or any taste at all beyond that of pepper. There was yelling and sneezing, and sneezing and yelling, and crying, and yipping, and peppering. The only thing that did not sneeze was the big cat sitting on the hearth. It was grinning from ear to ear.

Alice asked, "Why is your cat grinning?" She sensed something odd about the cat. Beyond its grin.

"It is an aether cat, that is why," the Duchess replied. "They are always up to something. Little pig bitch!" She said the last words with a sudden violence, such as made the baby jump considerably. Alice assumed, for the Duchess' sake, that the insult was directed at the child.

"I did not know that cats could smile," Alice said. She had heard tell of the otherdimensional aspects of such felines but had never met one.

"They do the most impossible things," said the Duchess. "And implausible things. And shrimp cocktailible things. And labia shovels, too!"

"I do not know about those last few things," Alice remarked. "My Nonsense-to-English is rather rusty."

"You don't know much, it is true," the Duchess snapped while pulling her lower eye lid down in a gesture of an unspoken, "Fuck you!"

"More like Bullshit-to-English," Weasel interjected.

The baby was still crying so the cook whapped it a few times on the head with a wooden spoon.

"What the hell are you doing?!?!" Alice railed at the cook.

"If everyone minded their own business, as well as those that don't but do it faster, everyone gets a go round of trade. That's economics. What a world," the Duchess said in a growl hoarsely. "Speaking of which, where is my red diamond tea that lovely Wolf person dropped off? The Queen of Hearts will not like the sound of that one, though it's the taste that matters. Some people have no taste at all."

"I'll deal with you next," Alice said, her patience clearly exhausted.

"Would be no advantage," the Duchess rambled on. "It goes on day and night, neverending, forever and ever. Crying babies, global economies, sleeping aquatic demigods. They all go on, forever and ever. You get the feeling that you get a chance to show off most of your knowledge, but you know nothing. You are a stupid little girl. It is very happy. You see, the Earth takes four hours from twenty to spin round on its axis. . ."

"Speaking of axes, I'll cut off its head. That should quiet it down," said the cook.

"Oh, just give the thing a violent shake," the Duchess responded. "Or sing it a lullaby, maybe a tune by The Miserable Ones. They're on tour, you know. I hope they play at the Banging Gardens of Babbageddon."

The cook started warbling,

"Pepper haze all in my brain,
over and over it's the same refrain,
tasting funny but I don't know why,
add some more my oh my."

And she worked the pepper grinder furiously over the soup in an almost pornoriffic fashion. Alice could not tell if she was singing to the baby or to the soup.

"I cannot comply with that number," said the Duchess. "Wow! WOW! WOW!" She hurried out of the room. The cook threw a frying pan after her but it hit the wall instead.

Looking to take out her frustration, the cook grabbed a meat tenderizer and was about ready to crown the baby. Alice instinctively reached into her pocket and grabbed the first thing she could to throw at the cook. She pulled out the rabbit's fan which she had tucked away in her pinafore earlier. Though small, it was weighty, made of folding ivory plates.

Alice let it fly and hit the cook square in the face. With rage in her eyes, she came at Alice swinging the meat hammer. Weasel hopped up a chair and onto the counter. With one good blow across the side of her head, the cook fell to the floor unconscious.

Alice pulled the baby from the cauldron. It was snorting and wheezing like a steam engine, its lungs filled with black pepper. It began grunting and twitching in her arms. "I think it's having a seizure," she said.

"No. They just do that. It's a temper tantrum," Weasel said.

"Oh, it's doing something alright," Alice said as she put the baby on the ground, not wanting it to roll off the counter in its tizzied state. It began to squeal like an actual pig. Then it began to turn into an actual pig, with tiny wings.

"Ahhhh! Werepig! Werepig! Kill it! Kill it!" Weasel shouted, then jumped off the counter and chased the pig around the kitchen, smashing what few pieces of dishware had survived the cook's earlier destructo tirades. "Look out, Alice! Look out! Werepig!"

"But, it's still just a harmless piglet," Alice stammered.

"Harmless? You really aren't from around here, are you?" Weasel stated.

"No. I thought that was obvious. This is all new to me, and I've been places, I've seen some shit."

Then the werepig began to squeal like it was in pain. It began to spasm again. Its wings grew larger and its hooves cracked and extended into humanlike fingers with full keratin cylindrical nails tipping them. And the teeth in its mouth became gnarled and jagged. This was not good!

Weasel kept in close pursuit but couldn't get a good swing

on it. As the werepig made another round of the kitchen it tried to bite Alice. She stepped out of reach of the squarling jaws and snap punched it in the snout. The hoof-handed horror did a half flip skid on its hind quarters then flapped its wings in a frantic burst that lifted it off the ground just enough to right itself.

This gave Weasel the chance he needed to catch up. He brained the pig several times with his bat. Blunt force trauma applied to the top of the skull decidedly and repeatedly. It was dead.

"Uh, this place," Alice bemoaned.

"Why don't you go outside and have a think, relax a little," Weasel said. "I'll make lunch."

"Good idea," she replied as she retrieved Rabbit's fan and headed out the door.

The dag dog had wandered off. Alice paced around the grounds to try and calm down. This was hindered by the surprise of looking up and seeing the aether cat sitting in the branches of a tree, smiling down at her. She swore its grin got wider when it saw her startle upon spotting it. She had been so caught up when everything went all higgledy-piggledy, literally, that she had not noticed the cat's exit.

The cat just laughed when it saw her. It had more teeth, and very claws, very long. Very, very claws. Though it appeared good-natured, she felt she should treat it with respect.

"Aether puss," she did not know how to address a talking

cat, as she had never met one before. Or any talking animal, before yesterday. And she had been back and forth through many timelines. "May I start by asking your name?"

"Cats don't have names. We just, are. It is people who name us."

"That seems irrational. Then how would one address a talking cat? As all the cats I have ever met could not speak English, or any other human language for that matter. And I cannot speak Cat. So they could neither tell me, nor could I ask them."

"You may call me Aether, or Cat, if you like. As the residents here all tend to gravitate toward the obvious. Most call me Cheshire, as I have chosen the Cheshire Queen as my human caretaker. We are, aetherically connected, she and I. As if a human could actually own a cat," he laughed.

"Very well then. How are you this lovely day, Cheshire?"

"I am superb. And yourself?"

"Very well, thank you, considering the unlikely circumstances." He purr-chuckled at this.

"You know there are rational numbers and irrational numbers, correct?" the cat asked. Alice nodded "yes."

"And you know there are real numbers and imaginary numbers, yes?" it continued. Again, she responded silently but affirmatively.

"Those are called complex numbers. There are also hypercomplex numbers. Well, when something imaginary becomes irrational, it does a quaternion quadrille, constantly changing partners in linear time and spatial reality. It is a subset in the group of abstract algebra known as metamathematics. But those of us in the know, we of unlikely circumstances, call it aethermatics. Do you follow?"

"Yes. Is this a lesson or a lecture?"

"Oh, it is quite the lesson. Had you not broken the rules of physnics then it would be a lecture."

"Physnics?"

"The laws of physical nature and picnics."

"Oh, yes, basket theory. I remember that, but it was some time ago."

"Sum time, indeed."

"And did you say, had I 'not' broken the rules?"

"Yes. Because rules are made to be broken. And you've broken quite a few in just the short amount of time you've been here.

Now laws, those are a different story. But let's move on."

"Very well," Alice agreed.

"The more irrational you are, the more rational your world. It's quite paradoxical, really. But we are the same, you and I. We are travelers. This is not our world. So while their ways here may seem irrational to us, it is really we who are irrational to them, which reinforces the rationality of their world. We are imaginary numbers in this place."

"So the crazier I get the crazier things become?"

"Yes. And that is perfectly normal. Here. Other places, not so much."

"So, like fighting fire with fire. Except, nonsense with nonsense."

"Ah, now you're getting it. The only way to stop the madness is to stop, then the madness also will stop. Nonsense begets nonsense."

"I am happy so far, with this place. The challenges have been tremendous, but welcome. Though their absurdity as a collective is quite perturbing, it makes sense as you explain it; in that it makes no sense at all. It is what it is, and that's all it can be. I am just wondering how I should go from here."

"It depends a great deal on where you want to get to," the cat said.

"I do not care, where as, there is not much to care about."

"Then it is not a problem which way you go, because you will find nothing for which to care about. That is your path, which lies amidst your apathy."

"For a long time I have taken that path. It always leads somewhere, for even nowhere is somewhere."

"Yes," agreed the cat, "all paths lead to nowhere."

They both paused in a melancholy silence. If your life is constantly going Nowhere, it can drive you mad.

"The path ahead splits several times," the cat said, pointing its tail, "more so than the personalities of those who reside along it. There is the Faelstrom Industries pandimensional curios and antiques black market, the singing rose, the Shardcore Shuttershack, Ravenscroft Asylum, the Chaos Pit agonadrome, ad nauseum.

"Mad, all?"

"Indubitably. And beyond remission or recovery."

"To walk among the mad yet not succumb."

"We're all mad here. I'm mad. You're mad."

"I am not the company I keep."

"If you wish. I noticed that you 'received' an invitation to the queen's croquet and beheadings party. Will you be attending?"

"Yes. Most definitely."

"Excellent. You shall see me there. I love crashing parties. Especially royal ones." Then the cat vanished quite suddenly.

She was accustomed to strange things happening, but this caught Alice by surprise. "Well, now I know why it's called an aether cat." She was still looking at the place where it had been, and it reappeared.

"Oh, by the way, though you are made of time, you will never have enough here. Just as I am made of aether, yet still I feel claustrophobic in this place. Time and aether are always in flux. So, watch your watch, as it were. Never lose track of time." And it was gone again.

Alice turned to leave when the cat popped back in again.

"My, you certainly make one quite giddy," she said.

"My apologies. It was improper of me to leave without bidding you farewell. The bad habits of the local populace must be rubbing off. Thusly, may I bid you assured triumph in your perilous journey ahead, for we both know it will be neither safe nor uneventful."

Alice curtsied, "Victorious adventures to you."

The cat smiled that mischievous smile and vanished quite slowly this time, beginning with the end of the tail, and ending with the grin, which remained some time after the rest of it had gone.

Weasel joined her shortly. He was carrying an ornate, silver serving platter covered in an etched latticework of hearts and roses. Around the circumference was an inscription, "Duchess, don't be a bitch! Love, Queen of Hearts." Theirs is certainly an odd dynamic.

"Fresh pepperoni pizza!" he said presenting the dish.

"Excellent!" she replied. Alice had visited countless realities in her travels, one often more alien than the next, but a universal constant that she had discovered was pizza. The style and preparation could be expected to evolve as such in a similar fashion, but it was the curious and slightly disturbing synchronicity that, regardless of a world's originating language, they all called it pizza.

Weasel handed her a tablecloth and she spread it on the ground. He sat the platter down, "It's still hot. Let it cool." He retrieved dinnerware and a pitcher of flazzle punch as a refreshment. They sat on the lawn and had a lovely lunch.

"What shall we do about the Duchess and the cook?" Weasel asked.

"Leave them be. We have Hearts to break."

Grin or growl?
Fish or fowl?
You'll wish you had brought a towel.
Growl or grin?
Owl or fin?
How'll you know what state I'm in?

They heard a jingling in the bushes. A young girl with two large bells in her hair and another on a choker around her neck came traipsing out of the foliage. Her outfit was simple and she wore a pair of goggles on her head. She tripped momentarily, then began playing a painted ukulele and singing to herself,

> "Half a pound of heroine,
> half a pound of treacle,
> that's the way the cake is baked,
> if Glenn will dare the eagles."

"Oh, hello!" she said, surprised but excited to see new people. "I am looking for a wild goose. Have you seen any about?"

"No. I would have cooked your goose, if I had," laughed Weasel.

"No, we have not seen any wild geese around here," Alice answered. "Why are you looking?"

"I have been given a list, see," she showed it to Alice. At the top was printed "FULL LIST OF ERRANDS" followed by the items she was to retrieve.

1. smoked herring
2. wild goose
3. jar of elbow grease
4. Brussels teapot
5. pail of tartan paint
6. Zorkian gruesbane

"My dear, I do believe someone is pulling your leg. They have sent you on a lark."

"Ooo, that Vincent Vostro! I don't know why he takes advantage of me. All I ever am is nice to him. He's a writer who has no friends so he has to make them up in his head then he writes them down. But he never lets me read his work. I don't know why. Agh, it is very frustrating! I'm Tracy, by the way. Tracy True, the Three of Bells. Which is why I have three bells." She giggled, jiggled and jingled.

"I am Alice Wardell and this is my friend Dirty Weasel."

Two curtsies and a bow later, "I saw the Cheshire Cat flounging (floating and lounging) about earlier," said Tracy, "You wouldn't happen to be one of those aether people, would you? I've always wanted to talk to one. I have so many questions."

"No, I'm not an aetherican, or aetherian, or whatever they call themselves," Alice said. "But I am a chrononaut."

"That sounds, important. And maybe a bit dangerous. What is it?"

"It means I can do some funny things with time."

"That must come in handy, as things are already rather funny around here. Funny as in odd or off kilter, not funny as in humorous or hilarious."

I know what you mean all too well."

"So, can you move very fast from place to place? That would

be quite exhilarating!"

"I can, but I only do so sparingly. It can be very tiring. And if you rush through life you will miss the best parts."

"Like the saying, 'it's not the destination, but the journey.'"

"Exactly."

"Um, I have a question," Weasel said to Tracy. "Is that a doll of yourself you have tucked into your belt? It looks like a voodoo doll."

"Yes, it is, to both. It is from the Tumera Peppercorn voodoo doll kit. Only I've added a twist of my own magic." She pulled out the doll, "Normally you bind a personal item from the person you wish to curse, but instead I've attached a lock of my own hair to bind the doll to me. A raggedy familiar of my own. I tied her hair up with a few blades of grass and added the bells and ribbons out of whimsy. Would you like to see me activate her?"

Weasel nodded affirmatively.

Tracy shook her head to jingle the bells, "Wake up, wake up, wake up." She sat the haversack homunculus down as it began to move. "Good morning," she always said to it, regardless of when she woke the doll. It turned and curtsied to each of them.

Tracy made a spinning motion with her finger and it pirouetted. Then she shook her hips and it began to dance about. "Very good. Back to sleep, now." She jingled her bells again, "Sleep, sleep, sleep," and the burlap babe stretched, lied down, and returned to slumberland. Do living dolls dream?

What is the definition of *being alive*? of sentience? of reality? Everything is subjective.

"I shall journey on and leave you to your lunch," Tracy said. "There are a hundred and sixty two ways to die, but only one way to live--musically." She began strumming her ukulele and "la-la"ing away.

"Bye," Weasel said.

"Farewell," Alice said, "musically ever after."

There was an odd shimmer, like heat rising from a boiling pot, that rose behind Tracy in a man-shaped image. She did not see it materialize. It looked at Alice and Weasel, made a shushing motion, then gave an okay sign and disappeared. Tracy had an invisible guardian. A tulpa, a conjured thing. Looks like Vincent's imaginary friends weren't so imaginary.

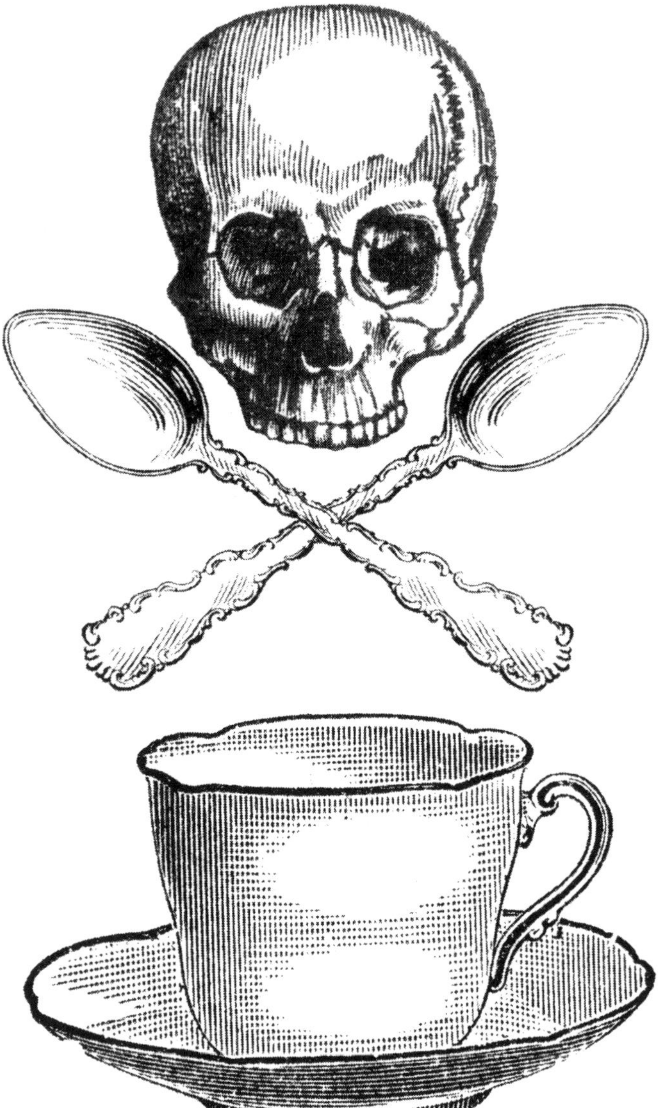

Weasel went a-romping
And running to and fro
Looking kind of worried
He said he had to go
But not from fear or frazzle
He had a whiz to throw
Oh, silly weasel
I didn't need to know

    Weasel returned, relieved.
    They traveled until they reached a fork in the road.
    "Hey, Weasel, how's it hangin'?" Alice asked.
    "To the left," he smiled and curtly answered, knowing her veiled question.
    "To the left it is," she said and headed down that path. It eventually lead to a large brick wall which stood ten feet high. They followed it around until they came to a pair of giant wrought iron gates that were hanging wide open. A plaque on the hinging pillar read "RAVENSCROFT ASYLUM" surrounded by filigree. Someone had scrawled beneath it, "HERE THERE BE CRAZY FUCKERS" in what looked like dried blood.

Chapter 14 - Mad Tea Party

    There was a trail of bodies leading across the lawn to a twisted and bent oak tree, underneath of which was a large table with a checkered cloth covering it. Numerous mismatched chairs had been set around in a haphazard manner. More place settings than persons who could be comfortably accommodated had been put out. Stacks of teacups littered the table as well as at least a dozen teapots of unusual shapes and sizes. The creamers had been filled carelessly and to overflowing. And there was twice as many sugar bowls than all the other teaware combined.

"Whoever killed all these people did a terrible job," Alice thought as she stepped over them daintily. "No one takes pride in their work anymore. Even psychopaths are becoming lazy and careless. Such haphazard strokes. No thought as to where the models, uh, bodies fell or how they lay."

Weasel trotted along behind, "This is a very untrustable trio. The March Hare and the Dopemouse are just sycophants, but the Mad Hatter is dangerous. Don't underestimate him."

"Why so worrisome, Weasel?"

"Wary, not worrisome. His madness is contagious."

"Don't worry, wary weasel."

Hatter and March Hare were power lounging while Dopemouse was fast asleep between the two of them. They were using him as a cushion, and as a napkin. The table was large but all three were clustered at one corner.

They saw the woman and the weasel approaching and cried in unison, "There is no room!"

Alice stepped up next to them and swept her chainsaw blade across the top of the table sending cups, dishes, and tea pots crashing over the side. She forcefully sat down her chainsaw in the newly opened space, "Now there's room," and proceeded to recline in the cushy armchair at the head of the table.

"Weasel, pull up a chair," she said, gesturing to her friend. While he did so, Alice yelled out to the others, "Tea! Now!" Dopemouse stirred at the sharp sound, mumbled something about "the untruths of baked goods" then went back to sleep. Weasel sat his bat on the table in front of him, but placed his violin a few settings over. He knew there would be trouble with this bunch and didn't want the instrument to get broken.

"It's not very civil of you to sit down uninvited," said Hatter.

Alice pulled out the invitation to the queen's party and slapped it down on the table. "I have been invited to play croquet with the Queen of Hearts. Any other lesser parties, such as this one, are considered open invitation. You're not refusing tea to a guest of the Queen, are you?"

"Of course not, my mistake. You had not presented your invitation so I was unaware," Hatter said. "Hare, pour the tea. Please. Please pour the tea. Now. Do it now."

"Jubjub jibber jabber," was all the March Hare had to say about it as he abided Hatter's request.

"What kind of tea is this, Hatman?" Weasel asked, sniffing at the cup.

"Manager's Special. A gift from a friendly passerby," Hatter replied.

"Was this transient guest wearing a hooded business suit, by any chance?"

"Why yes, he was."

"Don't drink the tea, Alice," Weasel said to her, then threw his teacup at Hatter. The majority of the tea splashed on the table, missing the mad host. This frustrated Weasel so he also threw Alice's teacup, this time soaking Hatter. And the tea was hot!

"I'll make a hat out of you!" Hatter said as he lunged across the table at Dirty. Alice leaned forward and gave the tea-soaked target a lightning left cross which sent him clamoring across the table and onto the ground.

"You must learn not to make such personal remarks. It's very rude," Alice said with severity. She leaned back in her chair.

"That friendly passerby was the Death Manager, you fool!" Weasel chastised the prone partier. "It's a sure thing that tea is cursed! The Bewitched Blend comes straight from the Macroeconomicon!"

"Oh, barbarous blatherskite," Hatter said, picking himself up. "He tweaked Dopemouse's ear, "Thanks for the help," but the sleeping sap simply brushed him away. He tried for March Hare but the ready rover bounded out of reach.

"You get what you get and you don't throw a fit," Hare said to Hatter as he rearranged the marigolds in the flowerpot centerpiece. "And you sure got it good."

"Suck a raven's dick," Hatter responded, crossing his eyes and sticking out his tongue. He stopped and turned, "Speaking of which, I know Dirty Ratzass, but we have not been properly introduced," he said to Alice. "Allow me to begin," he removed his top hat and bowed, "I am Hatter."

"Mad Hatter," Hare added. "And I am March Hare," he said, and tried to mimic Hatter's motion by removing his imaginary hat and bowing.

"Mad is subjective," Hatter said.

"You're subjective," Hare said. They got into a shoving contest. Hatter had the height and weight advantage so he easily toppled the flippant furball.

"If you're both done," Alice said in an authoritative voice.

"Yes," they both replied. Hare stood up.

"I am Alice. Chrononaut of the Transversus Infinum. That name probably means nothing to you. Keep it that way." Alice knew to stay in control of the situation, to maintain her role as alpha bitch. This was her tea party now.

"Hmm, that title sounds very important," said Hatter. "This calls for the special tea. Double tea. Hare, the infuser pot!"

March Hare ran and grabbed a teapot from the far end of the table. It had a tea infuser attached to the spout. He handed it to Hatter.

"Here in this pot we have Grand Panjandrum tea." He popped open the infuser on the tip and allowed Hare to pack it. "We shall add some Mad Tea, an exacting, but secret, mix of tulgey and sassafras leaves. Sweet, but dark, like me. My own special blend, don't you know. I love double tea."

He fumbled through his jacket pockets and pulled out a small tin. He open it and pulled out a dark granular object, "And the final touch, a Nonsensia sugar cube. Exhaustively created by compressing and sun baking sugar, honey, treacle, cream, unrequited love and toffee into a single dissolvable piece."

He closed the contrived confection in the external infuser and began pouring around the table, "The hot pajama tea, that's what we call it for short. Which is funny, because its short for long johns. Ha ha. Oh so clever. The hot pajama tea exits the pot via the spout and pours through the infuser instantly steeping the mad tea, dissolving the Nonsensia sugar cube, and landing in your cup as the perfectly blended double tea."

Weasel insufflated the steaming aroma, "seems okay."

"I assure you, it's completely safe," Hatter said.

Alice tried some, "Mmmm, quite good, I must say."

"Now that we have returned to a more civil level, there is still the matter of my honor which has been besmirched by your vermin companion," he said to Alice, then turned to Weasel, "Therefore, sir, I challenge you to a tea duel."

"Hahaha! A tea duel!" Weasel laughed. "You do know that I am the undisputed world champion!"

"The underground leagues and black market tea houses do not constitute a world which is acknowledged in the upper echelons of tea dueling. Your title means nothing here."

"Izzatso? Then break out the biscuits, 'cause you're about to get a weasel whomping."

"What is tea dueling?" Alice asked.

"You're about to find out," Weasel said. "Hare, set us up."

A fresh cup of hot tea was set out in front of each duelist. A tray of Royal Chessmen shortbread cookies was placed between them.

"Gentlemen, choose your weapon!" Hare shouted.

Hatter took a king, "I shall wear the crown this day."

Weasel took a rook, "Majestic, enduring. Outlasting all kings."

"On my count, dunk," said Hare. "One! Two! Three! Dunk!"

The tea duelists both dunked their biscuits in the tea. Hare counted during their submersion, "One! Two! Three! Four! Five!" and then they removed their sodden biscuits.

"The objective," Weasel said to Alice, "is to be the last one to eat your biscuit before it collapses into a mushy mess. If it falls in your tea it is a *splash* and you lose. If it falls on the table or floor it is a *splatter* and you lose. If it falls on your person it is a *splodge* and you lose and you are shamed. But the other combatant must still eat the majority of their biscuit to be declared the winner."

Hatter blew on his biscuit in an attempt to cool it and remove drops of extraneous tea, staring intently at the soggifying baked good.

Weasel shook off the excess drops and began weaving his

cookie around in various patterns. Though he danced about, his biscuit remained steady and level.

"What's the matter, Hatter?" Weasel said mockingly. "Your biscuit is bending. Kinda like your hat. Dance with me."

"Shut up, Wally Woodchuck. This is serious," Hatter said.

"Only a lunatic such as yourself would take his tea so seriously," Weasel continued taunting. "Lookie, lookie at my rookie cookie. Standing strong. While your crown is crumbling."

"No, no, no, no, no!" Hatter said as his biscuit began dissolving from the hot tea. He tried to eat it before it could drop, but to no avail. The biscuit splodged all over his jacket!

"Ooooooo, splodge!" excalimated Hare (which is much, much worse than just simply exclaiming; a excalimation is a dancing, mocking exclamation), "The shame! Ahahahaha!"

Weasel smiled a big weaselly smile. Slowly and effortlessly he ate the cookie. "Still undefeated."

"If you throw a fit because you lost and get tea on my dress, I will end you," Alice said to Hatter.

"Do NOT speak to me in such tones, little girl!" Hatter yelled and slammed his hand down on the table.

Alice jumped up from her chair and clocked him.

While Hatter was reeling, Hare pushed over Dopemouse and took a run at Alice. Weasel was across the table and tackled Hare. The two tumbled out across the grass.

"Hey, knock it off you guys," Dopemouse said and rolled over and went back to sleep.

Weasel pummeled Hare and bloodied his nose. He put his arms up and covered his face. He was done. Weasel got up and left him curled up in a ball.

Alice grabbed Hatter by the lapel and raised her fist. Then, with the adrenalin rushing through her veins and her sense of justice screaming to finish him, Alice gave Hatter a deep, hard kiss. "Fuck me," she said.

He had a look of bewilderment on his face.

"Fuck me," Alice said again. "Right here, on the table. I want you to go crazy on me. Blow your wad and what's left of your mind."

"Uhhh...okay!" Hatter replied and couldn't get his pants off fast enough.

"Alice! What the fuck are you doing?" Weasel shouted.

"That's exactly what I'm doing, Weasel. I'm fucking," she

said.

"No! I told you, his madness is contagious, don't do it! Or there's something in the tea!"

"I don't care, I just want to get laid. My choice. We're all adults here." She grabbed Hatter's now erect cock and started stroking it. She went down on him momentarily, then leapt up on the table, careful not to hit the cutting blade of her chainsaw.

Alice leaned back, lifted her dress and pulled her underwear aside, "Put it in."

Hatter did so and began pounding away at her as his legs hit the table with every thrust, shaking the pots and overturning the cups.

Weasel just shook his head. He grabbed his bat and wandered off across the asylum grounds. "You're not going to watch?" March Hare asked him. "I'm going to be hearing this story for years, so I need to know where the untruths and exaggerations begin." Dirty just waved his hand in a gesture and matching facial expression of futility.

Hare got comfortable on the lawn, holding his sleeve against his nose to staunch the bleeding. "Hey, you're missing the show," he said trying to rouse Dopemouse, but to no avail. "Stupid stoner."

The violent thrusting motion of Alice's mad lover caused his hat to topple from his head. She had to tell him several times, "No. Leave it," as his obsessive hat disorder made it difficult for him to maintain his focus, even on that sweet golden pussy.

"Harder. Fuck me harder," she said. He squeezed his eyes, and his ass, tight and doubled his efforts.

He put his hands around her throat, caressing, then gently tightening. She removed his hands several times, "No asphyxia."

When he did it again she unleashed a fist-blurring time punch, "I said NO asphyxia." He stopped to rub his jaw and try to put it back in place.

"Keep fucking," she said. He quickly got back into the rhythm. "Oh, yes. That's it. Almost there, almost there," she said. "Ohgodyes!" she screamed as waves of pleasure engulfed her body. She convulsed like she was having a sex seizure, a fantastic feeling fuck fit, the tremors wouldn't stop.

He was close, too. She felt his mad cock throb inside her, "Pull out." But he was lost in the ecstasy of the moment and couldn't hear her. "Don't come inside me," she said loudly. Still no recognition of the request. With extreme flexibility she placed her bar shoe on his chest and kicked him off and out of her.

He shot his psychocum all over her stomach, even from several feet away. His legs trembled beneath him as his pelvis continued to thrust with each ejaculative squirt. He took several wavering steps and collapsed into the nearby chair.

Alice was still basking in the afterglow and couldn't bring her legs down. She swiped the tummy cum onto one finger and flicked it into a tea cup. "You preferred cream, yes? Have some tea." The look on his face displayed that he was a tad put off by the idea. She found it hilarious.

The sensation finally subsided and she was able to roll off the table and sit back down in her chair. Spent and exhausted, she stretched over and grabbed the infuser pot, "This tea is pretty good."

Hatter pulled his pants up and retrieved his top hat. He stroked it lovingly atop his head. "Oh, I missed you," she heard him say to it.

Weasel returned shortly. Everyone had taken their original seats, except Dopemouse who had grabbed a table cloth for a blanket and crawled underneath the table to pass back out again.

"Where'd you go, whistle pig?" Hatter asked him sarcastically.

In one fluid motion Weasel turned and swung the bat down on Hatter's head, crushing his hat and fracturing his skull. Hatter's scalp instantly purpled and began swelling. A trickle of blood ran down from the brim. The mad man slumped in his chair.

"Is it possible to literally knock some sense into a person?" Weasel asked him. Though he had remained conscious, Hatter was too disoriented to respond.

Weasel snapped his furry little fingers then continually patted Hatter's cheek until he gained crazy daizy's attention. "Maybe, if your head's as cracked as your brain now, you'll be able to understand me. First, you try to give us poisoned corporate tea. Then you go into a tizzy when you lose the duel. You fuck my friend,"

"Ah, it was consensual," Alice interrupted.

"Yes. So you say. I'm sorry Alice, I thought it had been mentioned, the tea here affects humans and animals differently," Weasel said.

"Oh my," was all she could say.

Dirty then continued on with Hatter, "You drug her with your Mad Tea, probably the same shit the little doper rolling around under the table is whacked out from, and now, after all that, you think it's alright to insult me again? Call me a rodent again and you'll be joining the hospital staff out there on the lawn as the king of the corpses. You understand me?"

Hatter had regained enough of his senses to know that Weasel was not messing around and slowly nodded his head in acknowledgement.

"Here, put this on it," Weasel said, grabbing a butter dish and handing it to Hatter. "Butter will make it better. It is the best butter. Mind the breadcrumbs."

"Thank you," Hatter said humbly. He sat the butter dish down before him. He removed his hat, popped it several times to get it back into shape, then sat it on the table. He took a butter knife, sliced off a pat of butter, then rubbed it gingerly on the tender knot on his head. Though his hair was now mussed and greasy, it did make the goose egg feel better.

There was an insect-like buzzing sound, then a soft thwoom as the world suddenly turned a shimmering green hue. Everything was covered is a sparkly haze.

"Oh no, not again," Hatter said. "And of course, the one time I have my hat off."

"What just happened?" asked Alice.

There was a dwindling whisper like the soft tinkling of bells, and then it was gone. Faery laughter.

"We have just been glitter bombed," Hatter replied.

"That little pixie bitch," said Hare. "I'd like to see if her blood tastes like absinthe."

"Hare really, truly hates her," Hatter said. "Takes him weeks to get all the glitter out of his fur."

"Fuckin' faeries," said Weasel. "I share your pain and

animosity, Hare. If my violin is damaged we're going pixie punching."

"Much like honey is actually bee vomit, pixie dust is generated from the female faery's sexual organs," Hatter said trying to sound worldly and knowledgeable. It wasn't working. "So we have just been queefed on."

"It's clitter glitter alright," Hare added in support.

"Yes, quite so, Hare," continued Hatter. "It is produced by the glitoris then expelled by the vagector. Though they can normally control its discharge, some suffer from glitter leakage or premature enchantulation. This one obviously has no problems in the production department."

"The Queef Queen," said Hare.
"Quixotic erotic," said Hatter.
"Quirky."
"Queer."
"Quaint?"
"No, more quarrelsome."
"Queequeg."
"Quit it."

"Both of you shut the fuck up," said Alice.

"Such vulgar language," Hatter heralded haughtily.

"Vulgar? What is vulgar?" Alice asked, insulted. "I simply used an informal exclamatory interjection as a commanding adverb indicating the degree to which you should shut up. The fuck, that is the degree to which you should shut up. You should shut, the fuck, up. Very up. Very fuck. All shuts should be up and to the fuck, or at least the fuckingest that they can be. There are no four-letter-words only four-letter-minds."

"Worst. Tea party. Ever." Weasel was not happy. He turned to Alice, "We sure could use some of D-man's hydromancy right now."

"Undoubtedly," she replied.

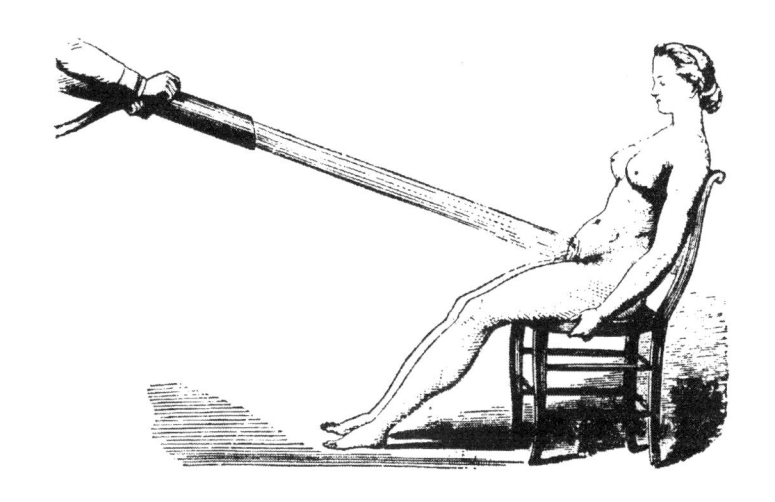

"Hare, go pull out that hysteria hose, the one they use for douching the crazy bitches," Hatter said. "We can try and blast this clitter glitter off of us."

"Where did you wander off to, when I was, uh, you know?" Alice asked Weasel.

"I went and checked out the asylum. I found an old blind dog working in the basement. His fur was singed in various spots, his paws scarred from years of touching hot metal. He feeds the furnace that keeps the steam generator running. It powers all the various mechanical medical devices in the building, in addition to heating it in the winter. They have pneumatic doors to lock down the facility in case of an emergency and pressurized air cannons for crowd control and riot suppression. Looks like their safety measures failed to keep them safe."

"Yes, that's Blind Shoveler," Hatter said. "We let him live as long as he keeps doing what he's doing."

"I know your grasp of the dreadfully obvious is most impressive around here, but what's his real name?" asked Alice. "He wasn't born with that name."

"None of us are born with a name," Hatter said, "it is given to us. Very inconsiderate, naming someone without asking them."

"Who cares, as long as he keeps the power on," Hare said, then left to find the hose.

Alice gave him a sour look, but he had already turned away. Weasel grabbed an empty tea cup and threw it at Hare, hitting him in the back of the head.

"Ow! What was that for?!?!" yiped Hare.

"For all the times that dog never tore you to pieces like you deserve, that's what for. Now hurry up with that hose."

Hare continued on his way, rubbing the back of his head.

"Do you think Shoveler will be alright here with them?" Alice asked.

"Yeah. I'll have another talk with our floppy-eared friend," Weasel said, "make sure he understands the consequences if anything happens to the old hound."

"Good. Were there any staffers still alive inside?"

"Well, I'm not sure if you'd call it living, but the terrible deed of closure is being taken care of as we speak. One of the patients who stuck around, Smiley Badger, is an old acquaintance of mine. We worked together before he was committed. I told him to go around and finish things up, make sure nobody was still alive and suffering. Put 'em out of their misery, that's what we'd want, so it's the least we can do for those poor souls. I'm no healer, no doctor, but they were beyond any other help we could provide them. I'll go check on him in a little while, see that everything's taken care of. You sure you still wanna go to this party?"

"Yes. It was a synchronous occurrence, getting that invitation. I could feel it as soon as I opened the envelope. Chrononauts can sense anomalous activities. Things that should not be."

"Like with the Yellow King?"

"Yes. We have free will, but the universe will give us a tug, or sometimes a boot in the ass, in the direction of the problem so that we can fix it, keep the time energy stream 'running like clockwork' as it were. And this place is majorly fucked up."

"So, you're like a time cop?"

"Something like that. I could just walk away, but I've found that the universe truly is cyclical. What goes around comes around, and it's usually bigger, badder, and much more pissed off by then."

"Let's get cleaned off and head out. We've got a party to crash."

BATTLE HOOKERS "ACTION" FIGURES - Chapter 15

It was late afternoon and the two companions were happy to leave the asylum behind them.

"I didn't tell you how the Jack of Hearts lost his eye, did I?" asked Weasel.

"No, you didn't," Alice replied.

"I was there, it was not a pretty site, though very gratifying to watch. The Queen of Hearts was hosting a rook-crook-book competition. Well, as if beating the queen at anything isn't risk enough at losing your head, he made an offhanded remark about the size of her ass and how the book would be safely hidden from the crook in her posterior. She demanded that he hand over his belt, which he did, thinking she was going to make some spanking or ass joke of her own. But she looped the belt through the buckle then slipped it around his neck like a noose. Not satisfied with just choking him and dragging him to the floor, Queenie called for the royal strap-on."

"The royal strap-on?" Alice pondered.

"Yes, a solid gold, ruby-encrusted dildo attached to a leather harness that wrapped around her waist and legs. The rubies had been carved to look like tiny roses. It was a splendidly beautiful piece of sex art."

"Go on."

"Anyway, she has one of the card guards hold Jack's leash while she straps it on. Then she takes the belt, pulls him to her, and proceeds to skullfuck him into unconsciousness. I honestly have no idea how he survived. The ruby roses shredded his eye lid and the part of his face around it and she pounded the tip through the back of his orbital socket and into his brain. The Ace must have been able to use her power to save the sonuvabitch. She is the only one among them who is actually true of Heart.

"The queen is bitterly jealous of her beauty and hates her with a passion. The king, though dominated by the queen, refuses to let her kill the ace.

"The queen caught Ace and Jack kissing in one of the castle's secret passages and had the royal barber surgeon remove Ace's lips and cauterize her mouth shut. She normally wears a medical mask to hide her shame."

"That is horrific," Alice said. "The queen must be stopped."

"We should devise a plan for when we get to the party."

"Yes. What type of defenses do they have?"

"Well, you met the Jack of Hearts. He is their heavy hitter. Though we sent him running, that will only cause him to ramp up his gadgetry. The card guards themselves wear a thick, layered paper armor. It protects well against standard medieval weaponry but your chainsaw should cut right through it. The queen doesn't. . ."

"What's that in the distance?" Alice asked.

"Oh, looks like Mr. Lo is back. That's his moving brothel!" Weasel said. "Let's go, I'll introduce you."

It was a four story building, walking. Locomotion was provided by six giant mechanical elephant-like legs. The steam engine which powered them sat at the back of the house, smoke billowing from the twin stacks. The cockswain steered from a second story helm, the bridge being nothing more than a balcony with a balustrade made to look like elephants trunks. There was an automatic gatling gun on the two front corners of the house, painted white to represent the tusks of the great beast, and a gazebo on the roof typifying a howdah passenger carriage. Painted on the side, they had christened the house the *SS Dickwhipper.*

"There he is, up top," Weasel said, then shouted out, "Lo! Howie! Hello, Lo!"

The man atop the house looked out and waved, "Hello, my friend Weasel! Come up! Come up!" Howie Lo was smoking a long cigarette and wearing salvar trousers (djinni pants) and a shirt with a printed mushroom pattern. He loved this area's mushroom forests and often partook of their culinary and medicinal bounty.

"He's from Warpaethea," Weasel said. "They're a very pleasant people. He has a full circuit of places he visits, making round trips. He always brings us treats back from his homeland."

"The girls aren't treats enough?" Alice laughed.

They both stopped. There was a shrill shriek approaching from behind. It sounded like the report of a rocket. They both instinctively crouched and covered their heads, expecting an explosive impact with the brothel. When none came, they both looked above and around them.

"We've got company," Weasel said, pointing to the figure now circling overhead. "We need to invest in ranged weapons at the earliest possible convenience."

"Not necessary. Find me some round rocks, about this big. They need to be as aerodynamic as possible," Alice said holding up her fingers about two inches apart. "I'll show you a neat trick."

Meanwhile, the mystery guest was now close enough to get a good look at. It was a woman dressed in the archetypal garb of a witch. She had a long orange skirt covered in a layer of black lace that billowed out behind her as she flew through the air. She wore a matching orange corset embroidered with a black leaf-and-jack (o'lantern) pattern. Her traditional pointed hat blew back from the speed of her flight. She wore a sugar skull mask over her face, goggles down for velocity protection. But instead of riding on a broom, she was seated on a long, striped candy stick.

"I thought I told you never to come back here!" she yelled at him.

"You're just mad because all the young girls want to work for me. So you have no children to seduce into your bed, then into your oven."

She raised her mask to better address him. "I don't. Eat. Children!" she screamed, hysterical with anger. A wave of her hand produced a hail of gobstomper candies that battered the side of the brothel."

"Bitch, you're crazy," Howie said crouching behind his lounging chair for protection from the candystorm.

"I am not crazy!" she screeched, her face flushed bright red. "You want crazy? Here's crazy for you!" She pulled out a large magic cherry, almost too big to hold in her hand. She threw it at the brothelmaster. It exploded in a sticky burning mess, dissolving the parts of the gazebo and roof it splattered on.

"Akak, get up here! We've got company! Bad company!" Mr. Lo shouted through the hatch leading down into the brothel. "And bring the swarmer!"

Akak, house security, came up the ladder to the gazebo and popped his head out, "What's the problem, boss?"

"Witch trouble," Howie said, motioning to the airspace invader.

Akak climbed up and out to the edge of the roof and launched a canister from the long-barreled swarmer gun. It burst open mid-flight and released a swarm of angry bees that befuddled and beebuzzled the confectioner conjurer.

She maneuvered backwards on her flying candy stick and in a single fluid motion pulled out and uncorked with one hand a glass vial filled with a sparkling red-brown powder from her bag of tricks. She streaked the contents through the air and blew a magical cinnamon cloud across the entire area, dispersing the swarm and choking Howie and Akak. Their throat and lungs felt like they were on fire! Neither could do anything to fight back, they were at her complete mercy.

"This one is perfect," Alice said, testing the weight in her hand of the nearly symmetrical rock Weasel had found. "Set the rest of them down right there, in case we need more." She held it up, extended her hand with the thumb up like a painter, then squinted sideways with one eye at the hovering witch like she was aiming down the barrel of a rifle. "Add a little chronokinetic acceleration and I have become the gun," Alice said as she threw the stone and it blasted away with the force of a fired shot.

The stone projectile struck the candy witch in the ribs just below her arm. The sickening *crack crack crack* of broken bones could be heard from the ground over her yelp of pain. The direct hit sent her dropping straight down. A barely audible, "C.C. help me," left her quivering lips.

A dark brown stream flowed around her. Was the candy witch actually bleeding chocolate?

But it grew in size and took on a snakelike shape. It streamed like a sentient waterfall as it hit the ground and flowed her gently to the grass. It then rose up and morphed into a large, solid humanoid form. The bonbon behemoth stood over her in a defensive stance.

    Before their amazed eyes, as she had fallen and lost consciousness, the candy witch had physically transformed from a strong woman in her mid 20's into a young girl of about 13. It was the same girl that had tried to help Alice by shooing away the mean animals outside of Rabbit's house.

    "Well, this changes things, quite literally," Alice said.

    "What do you mean?" Weasel asked.

    "She was in the crowd at Rabbit's, when I first met you."

    "I remember her! Are you sure she's the same one?"

    "Yes. She is."

    Mr. Lo and Akak had taken the opportunity granted by the respite and made their way down from the gazebo. Some of the working girls had come out onto the balconies. The cockswain had targeted the gatling guns on the two antagonists.

    Akak came rolling out, goggles on, ready for a fight. He had grabbed an oxyfuel cutting torch and opened the valve to its fullest, creating a long, thin flame. Mr. Lo came trailing out wielding a jagged Warpathian sword. Weasel stepped in front of the two combatants and put his paws up, "Wait! Wait! Wait! We know her, kind of. Cool your tool."

    Howie lowered his sword. "Akak, shut it off. What's the deal, Dirty?"

    "This is my friend, Alice," he said, making a quick gesture, "the little witch tried to help her when she was attacked by a mob."

    The brothel baron smiled and nodded at Alice, then the look on his face turned to puzzled then to one of recognition, "Oh! Alice! Alice with the chainsaw, Alice! The one who decap, feated, de-feated, Ritorubiru. A pleasure to meet you." He extended his hand in friendship to Alice.

    "Likewise," she said, shaking his hand. "News travels fast."

    "I must also thank you. Ritorubiru was a wicked lizard. Once an honorable warrior, in his later years serving the Queen of Hearts he became nothing but a bully and a junkie. Perhaps he always was, only he had been high on pride when he was younger, until that was no longer enough."

    "Yes, he was just another royal thug," Weasel added.

    "Any friend of Dirty Weasel's is a friend of mine. And by extension, the little witch as well. You are all welcome here. It is not just my place of business, it is my home. As for Cocoa Mountain..."

"Hmm, yes, let me try," Alice said. She turned and began walking toward the fallen girl but the protective chocolate elemental would not allow her to get close. Alice made a nudging motion, "Try to wake her," she said to it. The living confection acquiesced and gently tried to rouse his unconscious ward.

She was momentarily confused, then smiled to see her dark chocolate knight standing guard over her, "C.C. My protector." She sat up in an attempt to fully regain her bearings. That's when she realized the damage she had sustained from the velocious stone.

Her ribs were broken and her entire side was bruised from the impact.

"My spoon. My spoon. Where's my spoon?" she said as she rummaged through her bag, wincing with every movement. She finally found it.

She held the spoon aloft and twirled it above her head. With the nonsense magic words, "treacle debacle quixotic fixotic," she leveled the enchanted utensil and a golden syrup filled the bowl of the spoon. "Ahhh, that's better," she sighed in relief drinking it down as the fixer elixir healed her wounds.

"Are you alright now?" Alice leaned over and asked.

"Yes, thank you," she replied.

"I am Alice. I'm afraid your flying stick and mask have broken in the fall."

"That's okay. I can make more. I am Emulsa Tamworth, candy witch. Sweet to meet you."

Alice smiled, "It is sweet to meet you, too. I never had a chance to thank you for your help with the crowd at Rabbit's house. That's also where I met my friend here, Dirty Weasel."

"Of course! They are a perpetual vortex of agitation, that lot. Busybodies every one. Sweet to meet you, Mr. Weasel. I must say, you look very clean for a dirty weasel."

Weasel chuckled.

"Speaking of agitation," Alice continued, "what is your quarrel with Mr. Lo? Do you disapprove of his profession?"

"Oh, no, no. That's not it. Well, sort of. It *is* a shame that girls need to seek such vocation, but that is the way of the world. That will never change. Supply and demand. I'm sure Mr. Lo takes very good care of his charges, keeps them safe and sound. It would seem so judging by the size and firepower of his fornication fortress."

"Then what is it?"

"That monstrosity of a walking whorehouse keeps trampling

the flowers! It is disrupting the bees. Disrupted bees are not happy bees. And unhappy bees make unhappy honey. It is bittersweet. I cannot have bittersweet honey. I need it for my sugar magic. It must be sweet, sweet golden. Not bitter." But then she became irate. "And that bee gun! Give it to me and release those bees or I will summon up a hot fudge volcano here and now! I will cover you in gooey chocolate lava! Then I will make brownies from your choco-charred bones!"

"You want flambé?" Akak asked, presenting his torch.

"Now, now, calm yourself," Alice said. "All of you. I'm sure Mr. Lo will find it agreeable to stick closer to the paths and paveways."

There was a slight metallic clinking sound emanating from behind the group. It was hard to see the face of the figure walking toward them as the sun set at its back. As it moved closer they could make out a black bolero hat and an all-white jorongo. The jangling was from the spurs worn on the black boots.

His horseshoe mustache swooped into outrageous mutton chops. He looked like he had been plucked straight out of the American Wild West. There was a black spade on his jorongo over his left breast. He said nothing as he walked past.

"The Ace of Spades," Mr. Lo gasped.

"Something bad is about to happen," Akak said. "I'm gonna go armor up."

"Good idea. And get the Geargrinder ready. We'll need it."

"What's so special about this Ace that he can hold everyone in awe?" Alice asked aside to Weasel.

"He very rarely leaves Spadeland. When he does, it is usually on behalf of the Queen of Spades. Theirs is the suit of war. Wherever he goes, death follows."

"What's going on?" Emulsa asked innocently, not knowing who the Ace was.

He stopped but did not turn around. "Big battle," he said, then continued walking.

"Oh. I should find where my goggles went, then," Emulsa said, and proceeded to wander around looking for them.

The Ace moved over the next hill and was gone. Mr. Lo went inside.

"Weasel!" exclaimed a voice from the cockswain's balcony.

He looked up and saw his old friend, "Supera! Did you hear?"

"Yes! Akak just told us! Tonight, we FIGHT! Hahaha! I haven't had a good brawl in months. This should be spectacular!"

"You know it, battle bitch! And, with what shall you kill them, dear Liza, dear Liza, with what shall you kill them, with what?"

"For this battle I shall don my mechanical wings and the Firebird shall bring death from above!"

"Kill 'em with fire!"

"Yes! Sexplosive! The other girls are serving as my munitions crew. They're inside making firebombs right now."

"Droppin' f-bombs! Beautiful!"

"Okay, I gotta get back inside, check the wings, make sure they're in proper working order."

"Alright! See you soon!"

"So we'll have some help in the upcoming fight," Alice said.

"Yes. That was Supera. It's short for Super Pussy Fuck Machine."

"Oh. Is she part automaton?"

"No. She just fucks like one," Weasel laughed. "That's her 'performing' name. She is an entertainer, after all. The girls often use names they think are exotic and alluring to convince the johns to pick them. She thought the idea was foolish, since the men don't care about names, they just want to fuck. So she chose that one as a lark and it stuck."

"I take it from her enthusiasm and brawling statement that she's done this before. The fighting, I mean, not the fucking. Obviously she's done the fucking."

"That's how I met her; from the fighting, not the fucking, haha. The Queen of Diamonds was hosting an Orgy & Murder Party..."

"A what?" Alice interrupted.

"Well it was actually called the Diamond Ball, but any time the Card Queens throw these lavish parties, there is always wild sex and assassination attempts. Supera was actually a Diamond courtesan. They were called the queen's tarts, in mockery of the Queen of Hearts' passion for pastries. She was beating one of the card guards who had gotten out of hand, in the literal sense. Supera may be a sex worker but she will not be disrespected. We used the unconscious guard as a bench and struck up a conversation. We hit it off immediately.

"She always wanted to be an airship pirate. Heard tales about them in far off lands. Unfortunately, flying ships are uncommon in these parts. But we do have a few mad scientists running about, sciencing and what-have-you. So she saved her money, and probably threw in some free sex, and had a pair of mechanical wings built. This soiled dove can fly, and breathe fire."

"Breathe fire?"

"Yes. Her father used to beat her when she was very young, so she ran away and joined the circus. Cliché, huh. She was the Dragon Lady back then. Did an act of ballet and fire-breathing. One of the royal hangers-on of the Diamond court took a liking to her and had her brought in. She grew tired of the politics of the palace, beyond the fact that she had pummeled just about every maid and servant who thought they could talk down to her; so her welcome had been wearing thin for quite some time. That's when Mr. Lo happened to be passing through the province and she's been with him ever since."

"At least we have some aerial support. That can often change the tide of battle," Alice said. "Emulsa, will you be joining us then?"

"Yes. I can tell by everyone's state of alertness due to the presence of the card recluse that my assistance may be required to protect our homeland." She had found her goggles and put them back on her hat. She took a leather bracer from her bag and slipped it on her right arm. It had eight strips of beaten brass that ran the length of the arm guard with a raised muzzle at the wrist on each one. Weasel was curious to see it in action, thinking it was a magical projectile weapon.

A ramp door at the back of the brothel slammed open and out came a bizarre looking machine. This must be the Geargrinder. It looked at first like a giant mechanical pushcart. On further inspection, it appeared that Mr. Lo had built himself a two-wheeled, steam-powered, nightmarish road locomotive. The metal wheels were ten feet high, with the carriage and rear-mounted engine suspended between the two at the axle. It was literally hell in a handbasket. There must be a gyroscopic mechanism in place to keep the carriage level and balanced during acceleration.

The spiked heavy metal wheels gave it tremendous traction and the two-wheeled design gave it an incredibly sharp turn radius. The pneumatic tilt steering was simple and subtle but allowed for quick directional shifts. The carriage was open-topped. Howie sat center on the front bench seat while Akak was in the back. The carriage was high enough so that Akak could stand and fire weapons over the top of the wheels, and the gaps between the solid steel spokes allowed Howie to see out his peripherals.

The Magic Hallowe'en

All Hallowe'en, the magic night,
When folly reigns supreme,
The pumpkin heads are all alight,
The stars are all agleam.

Ghoul Parade - Chapter 16

The concubine combatants and the wondrous warriors all gathered outside the brothel, readying to move out. A cacophonic revelry was coming through the woods nearby. A cavalcade of nightmarish creatures was being lead by a woman in a harlequin dress and covered in a white shroud marked at the bottom by a large black skull and crossbones. A squad (squash?) of living jack o'lanterns bounced around her in chaotic step to the music. The ghoul parade stopped before them.

"Eep!" Emulsa flusterblurted and fell to her knees. "Her Majesty, Sahwin, Queen of Halloween."

"Rise child, please," Sahwin said. "Such terrestrial titles are superfluous. I am no queen. I am merely the embodiment of night, the spirit of Halloween, borne from the hopes and dreams of those in darkness. And when I am no longer needed, I will fade aetheric, and shall dance again with the Man in the Moon. But I will only be a wish away."

"Don't go."

"Not yet. I am very much needed, and that is why we are here. There are terrible things about. Corporate entities haunt this place."

"Death Manager," Weasel said. "A hostile takeover."

"Yes. He and his firmageists are destroying these lands. The Queen of Hearts, in her blind hatred for the other Card Queens, has summoned him here," Sahwin said. "He will fight in her name until it no longer serves him to do so, then he will turn on her as well."

"I am surprised that they have Halloween in these lands," Alice said.

"Ah, my dear, I have a million names. Many of the creatures here visit your world, but only at the witching hour, or in dreams. In this land they call it The Festival of Night. But we are all connected, Alice, each and every one."

"How do you know my name?"

"Young champion, I knew you before you were born. Yours is a truly unique gift, and you will become what you have always wanted to be," Sahwin said, and with a wink and a smile she emphasized the last part, "in time, in time."

"Well, I do hope to fair well in the upcoming battle."

"And you shall." Sahwin called to her pumpkin general,

"Jack Spit, if you please."

A bogy grabbed the called for bouncing jack and held it aloft for the queen. She reached inside it and pulled out a very small piece of paper. "Present your weapon, Champion of the Cutting Chain," she said to Alice.

Our heroine pulled her chainsaw from its harness and hoisted it aloft.

The Queen of Halloween said, "For bravery in battle," and placed a sticker of a yowling black cat which read, "I'm no scaredy cat!" on the casing of the saw. She whispered to Alice, "It's magic."

Emulsa was so ecstatic she was like a puppy about to wag its tail off. "And I have not forgotten you," Sahwin said. "I have a special flavor for the candy witch." She handed Emulsa a brass ring with a carnival tent etched on it. "I have seen your chocolate elemental, so you already know what this ring can do."

"Yessss. Thankyouthankyouthankyouthankyouthankyou!!!" she gigglesqueaked and jumped up and down. She had to hold her loose corset from sliding off. "Well, time to prepare for battle." Emulsa bowed her head then took in a deep breath and held it. With a wave of her hand she was surrounded in a vortex of swirling, magic sugar. She raised her head, eyes glowing red, "Feel the rush!" Her body transformed from that of the thirteen-year-old girl to a full grown candy witch ready to do some serious damage.

She slipped on the ring Sahwin had given her, then nodded in thanks once again to her queen.

"Now, to do a little sugar summoning of my own," Emulsa said, "I call upon all the forces of the Rock Candy Mountains!"

Within moments there was a rumbling beneath the ground. Trolls began to burst forth from the earth. Rock candy trolls! with mixed forms of flesh and crystallized sugar. Their shaman leader had heard Emulsa's sympathetic call and transported his legion to her aid.

"Though we have always offered to help Mistress Tamworth, she has never called upon us until now. So we know that she must be in a dire way, as is apparent by the forces gathered here. What do you desire of us, kindred sugar spirit?" he asked Emulsa.

"Wise Esocrux, a tremendous battle, one that can determine the fate of all our lands, is to take place," she said.

"Wow, are things really about to get that out of control?" Alice asked aside to Weasel. He simply nodded affirmatively.

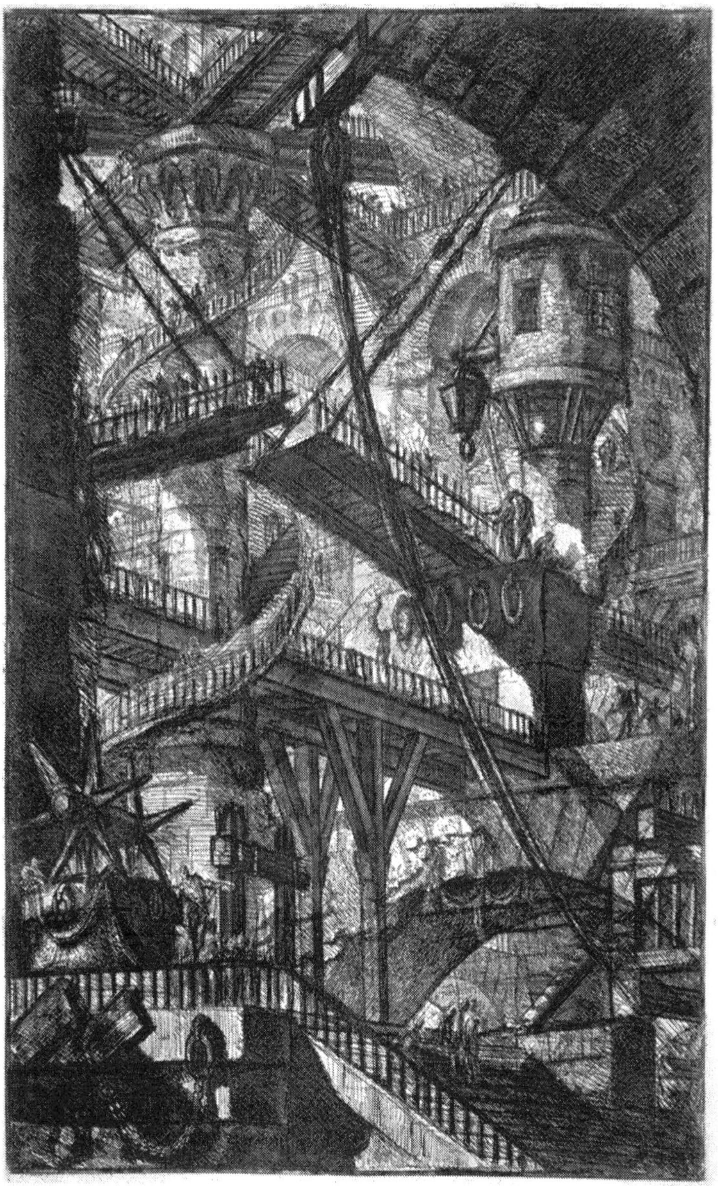

Sahwin stepped forward, "We march on the corporate castle of Wolfco. It is an industrial complex which scrapes the sky. One filled with the soulless slaves who have been pressed into service by the vile Death Manager. The battle shall be monumental, many will die tonight. Will you stand with us?"

"Yes. The trolls of the Rock Candy Mountains shall stand with you against this foe." Sahwin and Emulsa both thanked him.

"Hookers, trick-or-treaters, and candy monsters. Some army," Alice said. "Marching to fight the evils of corporate zombies. This place has an interesting perspective on reality."

"Don't underestimate," Weasel said, "those are a bunch of bad ass hookers. The brothel battalion carries serious firepower. They travel through some ultraconservative places where people like to impose their opinions on others. Lo has been forced to take a military stance on several occasions. Violence is the only language a lot of those types speak. His girls are fluent and cunning linguists."

"Now, denizens of darkness, ready yourselves," the Queen of Halloween called out to her followers. "My night things, it is time to go bump." All the cartoonish characters and whimsical will-o-wisps took on a nightmarish visage. Teeth and claws and horns. Sharp and pointy. Night renders.

"Well," said Alice, "perhaps they do stand a chance. We abide among this fluid, transformative landscape. Tell me, Weasel, have you every watched your friends die brutally in front of you?"

"Um, no."

"You may be about to. But I for one," she pulled down her goggles, "will not be among them. Stick close, we'll need to move quickly. Storming any type of facility can be very chaotic, especially with no prior battle plan or layout of the target. 'Go! Kill!' is not always very effective."

"Excellent point," Weasel said. "We'll use the trolls to get us inside the facility. From there it will be up to us." He turned and called out, "Emulsa. Bat strat time. We need to discuss our battle strategy with your troll friends." He went to confer with the other leaders of the group.

"Over the next hill. The future is always over the next hill," Alice said to herself. "Why is no one ever happy with where they are or what they have? Never living in the present. Lost souls, wandering lands, time wasted." She did one last check of her gear, then let Weasel know that she would wait for him over the next hill when he was done.

She gathered several more round rocks to use for ammunition and put them in her pocket. "I should be gathering flowers of peace not stones of war. History repeats."

Killing is my Business... and Business is Good!
Chapter 17 Bankruptcy

    Alice crested the next hill and surveyed the landscape. It was a truly bizarre industrial castle factory complex. Though located in a glen which nestled snugly between the surrounding hills, it had been sunken further into the earth. The ash billowing from the smokestacks was dispersed by either urban spirits or smoke elementals. It was difficult for Alice to determine from this distance.
    She hoped they were elementals. Though urban spirits have existed since the beginning of man's "civilized" age, it was not until the Industrial Revolution, when the terrible work conditions and the death of countless laborers fed the spirit of the age and the unclean spirits of modern society began to emerge. Darker, harsher, cruel combisouls; metro ghosts, polisneumas. Undirected vengeance, lashing out not at just the cities and corporations that created them but at any who crossed their paths or had the misfortune to stumble across their hideyhole havens, secret sewer sanctuaries, or underground urban cathedrals.

The Ace of Spades had walked down the hill and stood waiting in front of the corpopolis. The heavy metal bay doors had been opened and a rush of firmageists came out to meet him. They were truly un-dead. Living beings whose spirits are slowly killed. Though their bodies continued to function they could not be said to be truly alive. In fact, the spirit inhabiting the body was not really even their own, but one that had been corrupted, infected, forever changed by Wolfco's businessence.

Corporate personhood. The politicomancers knew what they were doing when they gave corporations the same rights as natural persons in the eyes of the law. The illuminating eyes of the law. *Dartmouth College v. Woodward*, 17 U.S. 518 (1819) was not just a "landmark decision" in corporate law, it was a magical tome written in the blood of the people, conceived by the Dartmouth Cabala Illuminatus.

Thomas Hobbes warned that corporations were worms in the body politic. But these spiritual parasites have grown out of control and taken on a life of their own. Forces of unnature. They have become living things.

The legion of firmageists did not set upon the lone ace, but merely stood in orderly rows awaiting authorization to attack.

A lumbering monstrosity came clankingly shambling out behind the throng. It was an amanu, a corporate entity greater than the standard firmageists. A miniboss, an executionary assistant, a psuepervisor--ugh, middle management!

They were easily distinguished from the masses by the corporate logo emblazoned on their flesh somewhere. It took many forms: a tattoo, a literal hot iron corporate branding, a glowing magical sigilogo, dermal piercings in the shape of the company mascot, etc.

This particular amanu happened to have a large rusty robot body with a living wolf head attached atop. It was a fairly primitive design, something you'd expect from hack inventors like Thomas Edison to bolt together. A boilerbot. More of a walking furnace with arms rather than much of a combat machine. Alice was not impressed.

The ace grew tired of waiting and pulled out two oversized revolvers. The custom leadspreaders even had a rotating mechanism for reloading that would move an empty cylinder out one side of the gun and another loaded cylinder in from the other side. With a pistol in each hand, in their own vernacular, he said, "It's time to eliminate the competition." He began thinning their numbers.

The high caliber rounds tore through enemy after enemy; one hit, one kill.

"Ego-mad fool," Alice said to herself, then turned and yelled down the hill, "Weasel! Sahwin! Hookers! Spades has started without you! Let's go!" She revved her chainsaw in short bursts to get everyone's attention then pulled the trigger as hard as it would go. She raised the slicer-dicer into a combative position and charged into the fray.

"Captain Mojave! Let's get this battle beast moving!" Lo yelled to the cockswain. "And break out the alcohol! Mojave's mojitos are the best, and if I'm going to die I'm going to die drunk!" He put the Geargrinder in motion and shredded turf up and over the hill. Supera grabbed her firebombs and took flight after him. The engine groaned as the *Dickwhipper* steamed into action. The other battle bawds were armed with various weaponry and stood on the balconies as the walking brothel trudged up the hill. The gunner was seated on a raised platform behind the cockswain. She had taken the moniker Bang Bang Betty and couldn't wait to get in range and open fire.

Sahwin, the Queen of Halloween, rose into the air and flew toward the battlefield. The night things went into a blood frenzy and it literally looked like all Hell was breaking loose as they flooded behind her.

The will-o-wisps pulsated and swirled amongst themselves

in a hypnotic pattern. These baleful bubbles bobbled around their queen like a defensive wheel with her as the hub.

Emulsa rubbed the big top on her magic ring and made her wish. An orange marshmallow circus peanut candy appeared in her hand. She tossed it to the ground and it turned into a giant orange marshmallow lion! The ring glowed as she used it to pull and mold a saddle onto the new steed's back. She climbed on and shouted, "Ho!" and the confectionary cat roared and bounded up the hill. Esocrux led the rock candy trolls under the hill. And the chocolate elemental trudged along behind.

The candy witch conjured a group of gummy goblins and commanded them to stand and protect her. She pulled a 12x8x3 inch box from her bag. She opened the lid which was on the shorter, narrower panel. She reached her arm in up to the elbow and spoke the magic words, "Pyxis of Siri El, show me the surprise inside."

She removed her hand as a golden glow burst forth from the box. A large, muscular Mandinka warrior materialized before her. His head was shaved clean except for a narrow central strip of upright hair which ran from his forehead to the nape of his neck. He wielded a pair of brass knuckles in each hand, but they were so thick that they looked like sledgehammers fastened to his fists. He wore a suit of fitted chainmail secured tightly with leather straps and like armor pieces at the shoulders, forearms, and shins.

He boldly announced, "I have been sent by Siri El, the God of Victory. What is thy bidding?" He bowed in respect to Emulsa.

"Um, run down there and kick their asses," she said uncertainly.

"The piteous fools shall be vanquished," he replied. Then he turned, descended the hill in a fastidious manner and joined the battle.

Alice was wreaking havoc on the horde of firmageists. With each heave and cleave body parts flew everywhere. And Sahwin's cute little sticker did more than give her comfort in combat, it transformed her implement of destruction into a spirit saw, a ghost getter.

The firmageists could project their etheric form outward from their rotting shells and even jump from body to body and reanimate other fallen foes if the physical wounds had been fatal but not too fractural. But now she could affect their businessential state. They were no longer untouchable.

And her custom combat boots were holding up nicely. Good tread. No slip and slide, which is important when you're knee deep in gore.

Lo's Geargrinder was tearing through the ranks, pulping the enemy beneath its spiked metal wheels. "Akak, bossbot," Lo said as he steered the carnage carriage toward the wolf-headed amanu. Akak turned his belt fed machine gun and fired on the lykos leader.

A blast of fire emanated from the furnace grate in its chest. Lo swerved to avoid being wiener roasted. The Ace of Spades responded with several shots targeting the lupine fleshing control unit but they were blocked by the lumbering metal body. Headshots on the head honcho were a no go.

Weasel joined the frickin' fracas with the night things. Claws cleaved. Teeth tore. The zombusiness meat suits were being slashed to pieces.

A dull thwumping sound could be heard coming from inside the castle complex. A terrifying site rose above the outer defensive wall. A mechanical jabberwocky, rotating blades replaced its wings to give the beastly bot its aerial lift. Plumes of smoke erupted from its steam engine. Its jaws were like crushing earth excavator power shovels with a prehensile chainsaw tongue. The industrial steel claws were as long as a man is tall and could tear through almost anything.

"They were waiting," Alice said.

There was a man in a business suit standing atop the castle factory's outer wall. He wore a pair of leather bracers over his jacket sleeves. The right one bore a control device. The left one bore a power source. Wires ran up both arms and connected at the back of his helmet. He had a communication device attached to it with the external microphone laying next to his cheek.

"Jabber-1 has been deployed," he said, "Let's get this rodeo rockin'. Send in the bullmen."

Supera flew in to meet the jabberwock. "Time to shine."

A low rumbling rang through the complex. With an echoing war cry, a large contingent of moneytaurs, creatures with human bodies and bovine heads, thronged through the castle portcullis and joined the battle, clashing with the multitude of night things.

Leading from the rear was the bald man with the dollar bull tattoo who Alice had prevented from doing harm to Joe and Patina. She should have known that letting him live would work against her.

"Initial perimeter has been established. Engaging crush/block secondary formation," said the eyes-and-voice on the castle wall.

A gang of four large automatons marched out of the factory complex and stood menacingly behind the battling bullmen. Dissimilar to the wolf-headed amanu, their humanoid form was sleek, artistic, like brass statuary forged by the spirits of Classic Greek sculptors and covered in etched Victorian filigree. Two exhaust pipes at each shoulder blade belched clouds from the steam drive inside the body's midsection. Their faces were smooth and featureless except for their eyes. Orange light from the internal fire flickered through their visual optic lenses.

"Strikers are in place. Send in the *Crying Skull*."

A traction engine with a railed platform atop it trudged through the portcullis. "CRYING SKULL" was printed on the side. The vehicle was white with black tears streaming down the front sides of the smokebox where the boiling water had run down from the stack and removed the paint. A woman dressed in business attire and wearing an armored trenchcoat sat at a desk perusing a thick book, its pages worn from age and handling. She seemed unconcerned with her wartorn surroundings.

Along the railing was a gathering of young females, mindless flibjibs. They were like cutesy harpies. Human in appearance, they wore babydoll business skirtsuits, stockings and sleeves bearing a winged symbol, and bar shoes. They had small wings that sprouted from their bodies in different locations for each fantastical femmefowl; some from their backs, some from their heads, some from their ankles, even some from their posteriors; yet they were flightless creatures. They could probably flap and hop about like chickens. But it was their incessant chattering, pointless gibberish, which took on an almost otherworldly air and became a mesmerizing cacophony. Odd birds indeed. They must be from marketing, most likely social media specialists.

One had two sets of wings and was wielding a spiked ball and chain of command. Her eyes were a mysterious blue. She must be the (scream) team leader.

The striker automatons were marvels of modern engineering. Built for combat. Any night things which came bounding over the bull wall of wooly warriors were struck down instantaneously.

The flibjibs fluttered about the platform and projectile puked a sickly yellow acidic vomit at any flying foes. They wore the wings of vitriol. Their bile blasts were so corrosive that some of the overspray had actually damaged two of the automatons who were too close to the *Crying Skull*.

The flighty females all stopped as the commanding woman stood up from her place at the desk. They began chittering in unison and made the unholy announcement of, "Lady Evarge' Dimensia, Inhuman Resources Manager, bearer of the Macroeconomicon!"

That book. That infernal book. The eldritch sigil for infinite money had been burned into its ancient cover. Destroyer of worlds by means of cosmic economics. Plutomancy, money magic. Currency is just another energy flow to be controlled. It can be symbiotic or parasitic. It can be saved or manifested. She was just like all the beings before her, Wolfco battle toys "made" specifically for this engagement. Special edition. She wielded financial power incarnate and would use it to drag around the kingdoms of this land and bend them to her will.

Lady Evarge' began to read from the Macroeconomicon. She was summoning a creature of mass destruction. Induced consumption had an entirely different meaning in her hands.

Motes of energy wafted up from the fallen bodies of combatants from both sides of the struggle. They swirled together and combined into the form of an innocent looking seven-year-old girl. She wore a dress as white as things that are very white; snow, fleece, flowers, fluffy kittens. Even her hair was an unnatural, crisp bright white. She was carrying a copper jack o' lantern.

The girl began to sing. The language was unknown but she projected emotion with every word.

"No!" screamed Emulsa. "She's souling! It's a trick! She'll sing for your soul, a literal life leech!"

Lady Evarge' laughed, "Who better to stand against the spirit of Halloween than a soul devourer? An exemplar of Vivulux the Living Light." Already various night things were giving up the ghost as they fell sway under her song, then dropped dead.

Emulsa pulled out a large rainbow swirled lollipop with her left hand and spurred her marshmallow mount. It reared back, roared, then charged down the hill toward the exemplar. The candy witch unleashed a blast of pure sugar magic in a gritting spray and disrupted the keening. It was like being hit by a killer sandstorm. The soul child's dress was shredded and her skin had tiny cuts in hundreds of places.

A fractaling burst of substantiated light emitted from the copper jack o' lantern and shielded her from the sugar storm.

Undeterred, Emulsa followed up with an acidic lemonade rain and the equally painful pun, "When life gives you lemons, burn a bitch!" The energy shield maintained its integrity under the toxic tart attack.

Sahwin smiled at the candy witch's bravery and tenacity. Though it was a powerful being, the Queen of Halloween had no fear of the exemplar, and allowed Emulsa to make her stand unaided.

The Candian conjurer presented her swirlypop and dazzling rainbow patterns churned forth from it. The tangible light thorns coming from the copper jack spun in defensive strokes in an attempt to keep Emulsa at bay. The Child of Fallen Souls averted her eyes to avoid the mesmerizing powerpop.

But the hypnosucker was merely a distraction so that Emulsa could get close enough to the little avatar. She aimed her brass-covered bracer at the wee wonderwight. Black licorice tentacles shot forth from the eight muzzles at her wrist. They snaked around the jack o' lantern and ripped it from the girl's hands.

A brilliant light emanated from the exemplar's mouth and eyes and mingled with the magic sucker's fascination field.

The battle brothel finally emerged at the top of the hill overlooking the battle. Alice recognized the gleeful maniacal laughter of the house gunner Bang Bang Betty as she got a clear shot and unloaded on the helijabber.

Suddenly! (Yes, I said it!) Suddenly, Alice was grabbed from behind. "What the?!" was all that she could get out.

She heard Weasel's voice behind her, "Hold on, this is going to be a weird ride." One of the rock candy trolls had picked her up. It jumped in the air and then plummeted below the surface of the earth. They moved underground through the rock and dirt and emerged inside the castle complex. Another troll carrying Weasel popped up next to them. Then the rest of the rock candy trolls and their shaman leader came up as well.

"But we can't leave them," Alice said distressed.

"We've got bigger fiends to fry, badder bastards to batter." Weasel replied.

"Yes, you're right."

"Lead, and we shall follow, Lady of the Chain," Esocrux said.

World's Greatest Boss - Chapter 18

    They fought their way through the winding hallways, spiraling stairs, and boardroom battlefields. The rumor that the basement was filled with lava trolls powering the massive steam engines of this fear factory was unfounded. The coal chambers only housed laborers who were there by choice and resentful of the insurrection. Some still bore patches of the Local 1251 mining union instead of their new employer's wolf head logo.
    The castle complex seemed to go on forever. Alice was not sure they hadn't gone in circles a few times since the entire place had not been designed for ease of passage.
    There was room after room of cubicles filled with firmageists in a dormant state. They could not distinguish if the throngs were being recharged by an unseen aetheric power source or

were being used as spirit fuel for Wolfco's ghostly machinations.
    Navigating the corporate maze, they arrived at the inner office sanctum. A large bronze nameplate read "DEATH MANAGER"
    "Real subtle," Weasel said.
    There was a set of wide wooden doors some 15 feet high. Locked. Alice started the chainsaw and cut through the door and around the entire handle. The severed piece fell to the ground as she removed the blade then kicked in the door. Opened.
    The cavernous office was devoid of furnishings save for a wall-high machine to one side and a Rococo oaken desk. One of the striker automatons was standing next to it holding a towel.
    A man in a hooded business suit, but pants dropped, was pounding away at a sexbot, a female human-shaped automaton with artificial breasts and a rubber replica vagina. "Come on in, almost finished," he said, his tie flapping to the rhythm of the smack of his thighs against its metal ass. "What is it people like to say? Fuck work. Quite literally. Haha. I love my job. Humanity and all its vices, spectacular!"
    He came inside the hobot and gave a few last thrusts. Then he pulled out, grabbed the towel from the striker, wiped off, and pulled his pants up. He balled up the towel and threw it in the corner. "One more moment," he said as he rummaged through his desk.
    "Dammit," he said, pushing the sexbot over and out of his way. "Move. Go. You're done." The coitomaton slid off the desk and left the room. He pulled out a bottle of cologne and sprayed himself down. "That's better." He returned it to the desk and closed the drawer. "The pseudo pussy is still a little, you know. Gotta have them work on that. Maybe grow a real one and implant it. The organic life sustaining machinery can be located where the reproductive organs would normally be. Imagine the sales then!"
    "So you're Death Manager, huh?" Weasel asked snidely. "You don't look like much to me. Are you actually an incarnation of death itself? Mister Reaper Man."
    "Death? No," he said. "But life, at least what you refer to as life, what is the meaning of it all?" He paused momentarily. "No answer? Poetically, that is the answer, for life is meaningless. Neither right nor wrong, there is no answer. Schrödinger's Paradox. Life only has whatever meaning or merit or value that any one individual gives it."
    "I'm sure you've got more to say. Continue with your

villainous diatribe," Alice said spinning her hand in a motion of continuance.

"Haha. It is the natural order of the universe to gather together. From our explosive separation at the dawn of time all we have sought to do is reconnect with our source. Cosmic dust became tiny one-celled organisms, which became more complex organisms, living things, which became the higher order of life you call humans, which became couplings which you call marriage, which became progenitors which you call parents, which became families, which became villages, then towns, then cities, then nations.

"Control systems developed to direct this cosmic growth. Religions, governments, armies, corporations, secret societies. Like a social nervous system for the entire planet. All species have a need to belong, to rejoin, and the control systems provide that.

"I am outside of all these things. I control the controllers. A holding company of the infinite, I invest energies in various realities. When you understand the true nature of the universe, and of life and its place within the grand design, you will see it for the nonsensical game which it really is. Would you like an ice cream cone?"

"Huh?" they both responded.

"Ice cream. Would you like an ice cream? I would. It's been a long day." He looked at the striker automaton, "Ice cream. Hokey pokey."

The menacing robot lumbered over to the large contraption with multiple storage tanks connected to a central vapor compression refrigeration unit. It grabbed a waffle cornet from a compartmented bin at the side, pulled a lever and out poured the ice cream from the frosted over nozzle. It then returned to the Death Manager's desk and gave him the cone.

"Are you sure you don't want any?" he asked. "It's quite delicious."

"No. We came to kill you, not eat ice cream," Weasel said.

"Kill me? You misunderstand how this works. For one, I am not just another of these random creatures who play at being gods. Theirs is a completely different game. Though, as I'm sure you can see where the different fallacies of the desire for control overlap. Once again, these are simply higher systems of reconnection. It is just that their policies and procedures are often in opposition." He licked the dripping cone.

He continued, "I fully research the nature of each reality I am attempting to control before I physically manifest in that reality.

This body is the pinnacle of biological construction in this space-time continuum. And though I do believe the capability to end its life functions are well within your ability, honestly, what would that achieve?

"I like this body. I am, *happy*, in it. It fits my energy signature well and serves my needs. And as I said, life is subjective. Why would I want to fight and risk damaging it? Besides, I have people for that." He finished his ice cream cone.

"Now, don't get me wrong," Death Manager continued, "I like you guys. You seem pretty cool. I'd like to keep you around. You add incredible value to the game. But we return once again to the subject of free will and your own desires to shape your reality and thus your own personal reconnection with all that is. If killing this body is the necessary catalyst for you to advance on an astrospiritual level, then go for it.

"But don't think it will be easy. And understand the risk of the loss of your own life functions. Alice, as a chronokinetic entity, your chance of survival in such a conflict is much greater than your terrestrial associate."

"Did you just call me a chronokitty? Is that a sexist remark?" Alice asked.

"No, I said chronokinetic entity. As in, a being who..."

"You must be an air elemental, because you're a fucking windbag," Weasel said.

"What?" was Death Manager's only response, perplexed by the change in dialogue.

In one fluid motion Alice reached into her pinafore pocket and grabbed a handful of round stones. With the greatest acceleration she could muster, they hit the Wolfco executive officer with the force of a gatling gun and knocked him off his feet.

"Esocrux!" Weasel shouted and pointed at the striker automaton as he rushed to take advantage of the prone powermonger. The trolls attacked the metal behemoth.

Weasel began pummeling Death Manager with his baseball bat. Which was quickly halted when the bossman took it and snapped it into splinters then grabbed Weasel and flung him back at Alice. "I believe this belongs to you." She was just able to catch him as she fumbled with the chainsaw in her other hand.

He stood up and began brushing himself off. "I was so careful not to get any semen on this suit and now look what you did to it." His chest was already purpled and swollen from the stones, his jacket and shirt torn. "I told you, I don't fight. That was really unnecessary."

The trolls used their strength and numbers to quickly dispatch the striker. But then they began collapsing. Alice lifted her chainsaw but her arm became shaky and weak, she couldn't keep it up. Weasel wavered then fell to the floor. Alice's head was spinning. "This is worse than the rapid growth bottles," she thought.

Death Manager walked around the desk and stood over the two protagonists. "It is a similar sensation to extreme drunkenness, but is less lethal to your liver. You will be dizzy and disoriented for another hour or so, then the energy sickness will burn itself out and the effects will wear off. Like I said, I want to keep you in the game." He walked nonchalantly out the door.

Alice forced herself toward the exit after him. Her chronokinetic ability pushed the sickness through her system and she was already feeling stronger. But when she entered the hallway Death Manager was already gone. "Dammit!"

She had lost.

DEATH CREAM CONES
SKULL AND CROSSBONES
TASTE AND SAVOR
INSANITY'S FLAVOR

Thgink Teloiv - Chapter 19

    After resting a short period, Weasel and the trolls began to feel better. "Okay Alice, let's head back down and see how the battle has fared."
    "If you feel up to it." Weasel nodded his head affirmatively. He picked up the severed lower arm of the striker. It was unwieldy but would serve the purpose of delivering blunt force trauma until he could find a better weapon.
    They retraced their steps and wound back through the labyrinthine complex. Upon reaching one of the lower grand staircases, Alice saw a positive difference to a familiar face. Sultori had obtained new, like-colored armor and the Violet Knight was born.
    That's what they were talking about! Those birds had not been so foolish after all when they asked if Alice had the wonders. She could see the wonder in her friend. Now she knew what they meant.
    Sultori and her colleagues had just finished off a group of moneytaurs.
    A slender male with gray skin and smoke emanating from his body stood by her side. His hair and eyes matched her violet shade. He must have been effected by the same faery magic.
    A gryphon stood behind them on guard next to a woman in a red wedding dress. The beast was obviously supportive of their colorful challenge as it appeared to have rolled through a berry patch in an attempt to dye its pomp and plumage a sympathetic violet.
    Would you look at that, reigning over the bullmen, insuring their end truly was met--the Nine of Black Hearts! A rogue card!

And she was wielding the Queen of Hearts' royal scepter. Well played, Nine.

She wore a suit of white leather armor in the ancient Greek fashion of a heroic cuirass bearing the traditional nine heart pattern, a pteruges with a black heart at the end of each strip, and a helmet with a black horsehair crest and her number name on the side.

"Sultori! I see you have embraced your change!" Alice announced loudly to get her attention.

"Alice! It is good to see you again! Perhaps not the ideal setting, but you seem to be handling the current situation well."

"As much as possible. Are you here aiding the Queen of Halloween?"

"No. Is that what is going on? An attack? We came here to discuss Wolfco's potential services. We know they're up to no good, but we needed to find out how much no good they're up to. And some of their products might be beneficial to our needs. We had just finished the meeting when all hell broke loose. Any non-personnel were automatically considered corporate raiders, so we had to start fighting our way out."

"Wolfco was attempting to take over various kingdoms as an agency of the Queen of Hearts. Multiple forces joined together to put an end to them. We just came from a meeting of our own with their Chief Executioner Officer, Death Manager. It did not go well. He escaped."

"Ah, the Queen of Hearts, that would make sense. Have you heard? The Red King has been killed by a marauder. He fights for only himself, he holds allegiance to no one faction, but he has assembled a group of armed rabble and is terrorizing the Chessian Kingdoms."

"Yes, I am aware. It is tragic."

"The Red Queen is in a fury."

"I would believe so."

The woman in the red wedding dress wept softly and said to herself, "Only he would call me Star. My little shining Star, he used to say. Now, my light wanes. I fear, my life wanes, too."

Sultori introduced the benign bride, "Alice, this is the Red, um, Mistress, of the Robes."

"You may address me as the Red Trull, for that is what I truly am. Why put on airs? But that is merely a word, not a name. I am Hovmastarinna, Red Lady-in-waiting. But please call me Hovma. Any confidant of Sultori is mine as well."

"Thank you," the Violet Knight said and bowed slightly, as much as you can bow in a suit of full platemail.

"Build, conquer, or steal, we shall get you a Violet Kingdom yet," Hovma said with a smile.

Alice acquainted Sultori with Weasel and the rock candy ruffians, and she did the same in turn with the rest of her party. "My Ashen companion, Sonam, has befallen the same mysterious alteration as I," she then motioned toward the gryphon, "and Haxor would like to, as you can see. His brother Hijakra fetches for the Queen of Hearts, but is quite unconcerned with her authority. It really is quite humorous seeing her try to chastise a sleepy gryphon." Then she gestured to the card warrior, "Nine has taken up the fight against her former matriarch."

"A fine band you have assembled," Alice said. "And what is that incredible piece of destruction you wield?" she asked of the weapon in her hand which seemed to shimmer even here in this gloomy, smoke-choked place.

"A vorpal sword. You wouldn't believe the number of mudstars and chumspikers I had to fight through to get it. Former owner was a jager dragon. Messy in so many ways, but its blood boils down to a wonderful gelatinous dessert."

"Sounds yummy!" Alice said. "You'll have to save me some. But in the meantime, we need to get downstairs to see if our friends need any help. We will have tea together soon."

"Definitely!" The two gave departing hugs and each group went their own way.

As an afterthought, Sultori turned and called out, "Alice! About your friend with the rusting heart, seek out Dexin the beaver librarian, he built and runs the Lodge of Learning. He's drafted a census of the residents and their occupations of the surrounding kingdoms. There's bound to be a mad scientist or automaton builder listed in there that can help her."

"Thank you!" Alice responded.

"And if that doesn't work," Nine said, "break the Ace of Hearts' arm and make her do it. Let me know if you need any help with that."

When they were out of earshot, Weasel chuckled, "I know why they were here. The Red Trull has a sentient venereal disease living inside her. They were probably trying to see what the Wolfco labs could do for her. I've heard tales of its anger when her host body is threatened. It comes out and--wow! Look out!"

"Romance is dangerous. Love kills."

Lady Evarge' was approaching through a low archway. Her jacket was charred, her armor was shattered in several places and dangled off her body. She still bore the Macroeconomicon.

A badly damaged striker walked behind her. Probably the only automaton that made it through in one piece. Several flustered flibjibs flanked behind.

The most pronounced member of her ragtag group must have been summoned during the heat of battle, a monstrous lemmek. It was a huge, semiaquatic, bipedal avioid creature with a deathly sharp beak and ornately carved tusks sprouting upwards. It had talons for hands and feet. The creature's hair had a seaweed appearance and was so long it dragged on the ground.

Alice presented her chainsaw.

"Look what we have here," Lady Evarge' said, "collateral drama. Is this the route you truly want to pursue, or would your time be better spent helping your friends? Well, what's left of them." A grim smile and questioning look crossed her face with ghoulish delight. "You may pass unmolested. A temporary truce."

"Very well," Alice said as she lowered the chainsaw. "Tending to my friends is more important than killing you--right now, at least."

"If looks, aye doll? If looks," the Wolfco warrior said. "We're not so different, you and I. See you in one hell or another."

The two war parties continued on their separate ways. The striker walked backwards and kept an optic on them.

They exited the castle and were nearly bowled over by Emulsa's huggy greetings. "Wedidit! Wedidit! Wedidit!" she blurted. "We defeated the Wolfies! I candy crushed that Jerkwerx! I even had that book in my licorice tentacles but she conjured up this beaky, tusky thing that got in the way. But I did defeat that Vi, Vivu," she thought for a moment, but still got it wrong, "Vivalulu battle angel! See! I got her magic jack o' lantern! Spoils of war, you know. Thinking about it now, afterwards, it was kinda offputting to see a little girl explode in a burst of flitting souls. I guess she wasn't really real at all. Meh, she's gone. That's what matters. I win!"

"Good work, Emulsa!" Alice said, finally able to get a word in edgewise. Weasel gave her a congratulatory pat on the arm. The rock candy trolls gathered around her.

Esocrux picked her up on his shoulder, "Hail the conquering candy queen!" She giggled and giggled while they cheered her.

"Let's go check on everyone else," Alice said to Weasel.

Supera was examining her mechanical wings. "How goes it?" Alice asked.

"Battle damage is to be expected. Definitely fixable. You missed it, Alice! I blitzbombed that flying jabberwocky! Took that fucker out! Yeah! It blasted Lo's wheels, but him and Akak are okay. Just a few scratches."

"How are the rest of the girls?"

"Oh, fine, fine. They were safe inside the brothel. Betty kept those corporate zombies well ventilated. Captain's working on one of the leg actuators that's sticking now. How'd you do? Did you get the head bastard?"

"No. He hit us with a radiating agent and made his exit while we were incapacitated."

"Whoa. At least he didn't kill you while you were out of it."

"Yeah. He said something like, life is just a game and it was more fun having us around."

"Weird cosmic entities."

"Indeed."

"What happened to all the night things?" Weasel asked.

"Their queen did some Hallowitchery and the bodies of their

dead dissolved. Then they stormed through the gates. They should still be in their causing chaos somewhere. Surprised you didn't see 'em. We were kicking ass, but she was the real turning point. The Ace was blasting away. Emulsa took out the little light girl, then she and her candy army just started laying waste to that bitch with the book. That guy she pulled out of her magic box," Supera snickered as she said *magic box*, "he ran up to the traction engine and straight up punched it, disabling the whole damn thing! Then Queenie's eyes glowed and the night things went berserk! Those will-o-wisps turned into these freaky energy creatures and just annihilated anything that came up against them. That's when book bitch realized that she couldn't win so she retreated. She was dropping sloars, bandersnatches, pokeyslokes, bitey klobbs, charczars, even a giant tanzerpanz, anything she could put between us and her."

    "It sounds like a hard fought victory, but we won," Alice said. "If we're not needed here, we're going back on the warpath. We've got a date with the Queen of Hearts for tea and terror."

    "Nah. Here's control," Supera said holding out her hand. "Here's us," she followed by placing her other hand below the first.

    "Excellent," replied Alice. "Then we'll be going."

    "No rest for the wicked," said Weasel.

My Knight in Stolen Armor - Chapter 21 (x2, eh)

      A thin young man was sitting against a tree looking up at the night sky. His hair was a light ashen gray, very unusual for someone his age. He wore a pair of pink translucent dice on a necklace, the single pip on each was replaced by a star. He wore black pants and a gray shirt with a black vest. His matching gray jacket was the vanguard of fashion.
      A nubile, pink woman was lying against his chest. Everything about her was pink. Her skin, hair, and eyes. Her scant wardrobe. Even the wraps around her legs which were printed in a

darker rose color with an unidentifiable ancient writing that seemed to hold a special or possibly religious significance.

Dame Sultori had explained that Chessians were born of varied skin color, but their hair and eyes were always of their birth color. The chroma of their people would increase in the skin tone of some as they aged. Some would not. Those born all solids of their inherited hue were of noble blood.

The Red and White Chess Kingdoms were bitter enemies. She must be a Pink Princess, of mixed race and hidden away to avoid bringing shame upon her house. Alice wondered if she might actually be the daughter of the Red King and the White Queen who had just been killed.

Regardless, Alice empathized with her flight from isolation and judgment.

"I haven't seen the moon in twelve years," he said as he pondered the glowing orb.

"What do you mean?" she asked.

"All I've known my entire life has been fighting. I began training when I was six."

"Six?"

"Yes. I was chosen to join the somuku when they

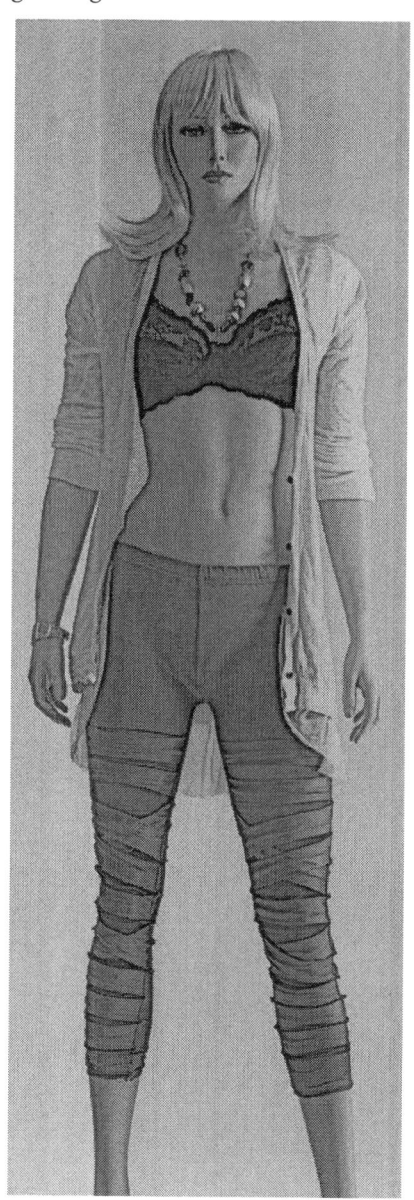

discovered my developing tychokinetic abilities. The night before I left home to learn the ways of the somuku there was a full moon festival. I sat up half the night just staring at it, until I fell asleep on the big hill overlooking my village."

Alice inserted herself into their conversation, "Probability manipulator, huh?" The young man pushed forward and began to draw his sword. "No need," she said. "We're not here to fight." Then she introduced herself and her guiding pal, "I am Alice. This is Dirty Weasel."

He returned his blade to rest. "I am Konton. This is, Shiroaka."

"A pleasure," Alice said, realizing his momentary pause was for him to manufacture a false name for her, to protect her. She's definitely a runaway.

"They call me lots of names; edger, kismeteer, last chance man, lucky bastard." He held forth his necklace and smiled, "I like dicer best."

"I'm a chrononaut, so we both play a similar game with the laws of physics," Alice said. "We're heading to the Queen of Hearts' croquet party tomorrow to let her know the rules have changed. You may journey with us, if you like."

"I have my own queen to protect," Konton said, then pulled Shiroaka closer.

"Good move," Alice replied.

"I have nothing left to achieve in these lands. We are heading south to Candia, probably Butterscotia."

"The Candylands are nice. You'll like it there," Weasel added. "You can take life slow and easy, enjoy it."

"That's the idea," Shiroaka said as she looking lovingly at Konton.

"We shall leave you to your peace and solitude," Alice said. "I hope you find a safe home in Candia."

Farewells were shared and they left the couple alone to enjoy the moonlight.

As morning broke, they came across an odd looking wooden construction, like a giant box with various size holes cut in it and pegs pounded in randomly. Boulders had been placed haphazardly about a freshly mown area of grass in front of it.

"What is this?" Alice asked.

"It's technically a shrine to Nafjaroar, troll goddess of

chance and strife. She is a sea hag who rules over those who suffered a watery death, the draugar, who rise from their watery graves to attack the living. Her name literally means 'corpse fjord.' They pay tribute by playing a lawn game that is a combination of life-size pinball and full contact golf."

"So they have a religion of recreation?"

"That is what it has degenerated to in modern times."

"Sounds like fun. How often do they play?"

"It varies. They're semi-nomadic, normally sleeping on the beach along the Diamond Coast where they can commune with their sea goddess. Then they go on random pilgrimages, set up these shrines, play their holy games, then move on."

"Look here!" Alice said reaching her hand through one of the lower openings in the goal box. She pulled out a croquet mallet covered in trollish runes and passed it to Dirty. Then she pulled out a leather-bound book (curious of what race or species the hide was provided by in a land of sentient, evolved animals that maintained their food chain eating habits). The silver characters *Mo Bé Deek* were etched on the front.

"What's it say?" asked Weasel.

"It's a mix of Celtic and Gaelic," Alice said. "Basically it says, 'Behold! My Grave.'" On the title page in plain English it read *The Wailing of the Wight*. The rest was in the same bastardized language as the cover. But there were margin notes in the trollish language. She flipped through the rest of the book. "It would appear to describe how to raise the dead from the watery depths in which they lie eternal. Makes sense for a group that worships a sea witch. Wonder if they're enemies or allies of the various Cthuloid groups. It's worth keeping hold of, at any rate."

Alice opened her satchel and started moving things around to make room for the book. She pulled out the picture frames which were acquired during her rabbit hole descent. "Recognize any of them?" Alice asked, showing them to Weasel.

He looked them over. "This one." He held up a picture of a woman in a commanding officer's uniform. "See the tattoo on her arm. This is the 3 of Stars. Their kingdom was destroyed and absorbed by the Hearts. Survivors were forced to change suit. Some fled. But I haven't seen any Stars in years."
"What happened to her, do you know?"
"No idea."
"Well, very soon the Queen of Hearts and her reign of tyranny will be only a memory." She finished repacking and they were off again.

They moved along the unpaved road through the lush but not-especially-descriptive forest. "I never got a chance to ask him," Alice said, "does Thomas actually want to go back home? I didn't get the impression he cared or was trying very hard in that vein."
"I asked him that myself before," Weasel replied. "He said our world was much more interesting than his. There wasn't really anything tying him there. Said his parents were his parents, but it wasn't like they'd miss him if he never returned. Apparently the bourgeoisie of his era tend to be heavily medicated."

"Look over there," Alice said and pointed. There was a clapboard building nearly swallowed up by the forest.

"I recognize the building, but not the newer sign," Weasel said. "The I. B. Loveless - Attention Society. That's the old mining hall for the Local 1251. Never heard of the Attention Society."

"I'm thinking they never got the attention they needed. Judging by the condition of the building, at least."

"It was initially abandoned because the iratathyst they were mining was making everyone sick. The entrance to the mine is actually in the hall."

"That's odd. I've never heard of that practice."

"They were very paranoid about people trying to steal the crystals."

"There's something else about that place."

"Uh oh."

The wooden door was rotting off the hinges so their access was not blocked. They rummaged about the hall.

"Here's what was demanding my attention." Alice picked up a metal disc that was two inches around. She held it up so Weasel could see it. "Time coin," she said.

"Time coin?"

"Yep. Go ahead and state the obvious."

"Time is money?"

"Exactly. A cosmic coinage joke, albeit not a very good one."

"Think it was Death Manager's, or someone else's from Wolfco? Money magic is their thing. Or maybe the trolls had been using it as a game token, dropped it when then came through."

"Possible, but doubtful. See these," Alice displayed the coin, "the thin lines are the original stamping. The thicker lines are a cthonic symbol and were marked over the authentic ones."

"What's it for?"

"Numerous things. As a focus to aid in time jumping, it can act as an anchor for a dimensional gate, paying karmic debt, accessing akashic records, Lady Evarge' probably could have used it in conjunction with the Macroeconomicon and obliterated everyone on that battlefield. The new sigil has probably been masking its presence from Wolfco. Not that they're in a position to do anything about it right now anyway."

Weasel turned his head.

"I hear it, too," Alice said. "Out back." She put the coin in her nacelle. They exited through the rear.

There was a blonde-haired man outside searching through the equipment and other refuse left behind. He was dressed like a zeppelin jockey and moved with an American swagger. The Davy Crockett emulator was accompanied by a young Asian woman wearing comfortable clothes accentuated by her aviator goggles, scarf, and winter coat. The weather was much too fair for such a coat. Her portmanteau was covered in travel destination patches.

They could barely hear what the woman was going on about, "Then I said to him, 'I'm totally down for lounging around all weekend watching a *Doctor X* marathon, ordering pizza, and lazy sex on the couch. But not every weekend.' So there I was, naked with a flamethrower..."

Alice did not mind interrupting, "Well, if it isn't Jenny Everywhere. If I didn't already know who was responsible for this place's temporal tomfuckery I'd think you had something to do with it."

"Excuse me? Who the smell are you?" she responded.

"Figures. Infinite lifespan, limited memory. Tambov. 1870. The northern Russian wastelands near the Arctic Ocean."

"The Icy Abyss." She shivered. "I, yes, I remember."

"I should literally knock you into next week," Alice growled.

"Ladies, ladies," said the zep jock, "let's not fight."

"Wherever she goes she brings a monkey with her," Alice said.

"Hey! What's that supposed to mean?" exclaimed the aeronaut.

"Yeah," added Weasel. "You seem to have this animal hangup." She rolled her eyes and gave Dirty a "not now" look.

"You're just a patsy," Alice said to the

high flyer. "Someone to put between her and trouble, because it inevitably finds her."

Jenny got in Alice's face, "He's my friend. My adventure buddy. My commando compadre. My..."

"...meat shield," Alice cut in. "Tell it to the dead girl, Aksinya Repon."

"She, she died?" Jenny stuttered then put her hand to her mouth in astonish.

"Just wait a min..." fly boy's chivalrous rescue was cut short as hundreds of thin tendrils wrapped around his entire body and pulled him off his feet! They began to take shape into semi-humanoid spaghetti monsters!

"Bobby!" the hepster yelled and tried in vain to pull him free.

"Get out of the way," Alice said and pushed Jenny aside, a tad harder than she should have. "This place just keeps getting weirder and weirder." She pulled out her chainsaw and fired it up.

A tangle of noodle tentacles ensnared Alice, but the baneful bowlful of awful food fiends were no challenge. "Hey Weasel, got any

Parmesan cheese?" she joked.

"Do they have red sauce for blood?" he asked cheekily, hungrily.

"No. I think they're more like animated or elemental pasta people rather than actual living noodlers."

"Ugh. My apologies," said a voice in the distance. A beautiful olive-skinned women approached them. She wore a wine-colored stola and limbus. "I am a goddess of feasting, not fighting. This is such a terrible terrene."

"Of course, madam. No apologies needed. Your observation is most astute. Allow to me to introduce myself. I am Alice Wardell of the Transversus Infinum. This is my associate, Mister Weasel."

"I am Edesia, goddess of food, divine spirit of banquets. I have unfortunately been summoned here by some halfwit incarnation of Snae Varath. These new gods are just a fad. As their popularity grows so does their power. But the fickle cultures that created them soon enough condenses them to cults, or forgets them all together and they simply fade away back to the aether. And who are your other companions?"

"No companions of mine, I assure you," Alice replied.

"I am Jenny Everywhere, pleased to meet you."

"And I am Robert Cambio," the aeronaut said with an arrogance that denied he had just been accosted by limp noodle golems. As an aside to Jenny, "Commando compadre?" She just smiled and blushed.

"Cambi Comcom," she slipped in, then stifled a giggle.

Weasel had pulled out a fork and begun tasting the leftover "bodies." He was overheard talking to himself as he went through his bag, "I've gotta have some hot sauce in here somewhere."

"Well, would any of you know the whereabouts of said Snae Varath by chance?" Edesia asked.

Only Alice could answer in the affirmative, "Yes. A few miles west of here. But that was two days ago. I met him momentarily on the road in transit. He could be anywhere by now."

"Thank you. I shall continue my search," she said, then returned from whence she came.

"Another time," Alice promised Jenny.

"Spaghetti Girl versus the Meat God, that should be an interesting food fight," Weasel said as they left.

"Weirder and weirder," Alice said.

Alice and Weasel came to a rickety two-story shack. A man with wavy shoulder-length hair and wearing a black dressing gown with a turquoise Narkonian lizard on the front left side was sitting on the large porch at a table having brunch. A suit of Tesla powered armor sat in a disorganized pile beside him.

A huge furry hominid creature was curled up sleeping on the grass next to the porch step.

"By the stair, that's Jurrus, he's a superbeast, a night thing champion who hunts jabberwocks," Weasel said. "He won a trophy for Best in Battle, if that means anything. It must be important to some people, otherwise they wouldn't give out such awards. They call him Hungry Hands, or Horror Hands, because he has a terrible toothy maw in the palm of each hand. He can wrap his long fingers around a man's head and eat his face off in one bite with those mouthy meat hooks. Feed the hand that bites."

A pet tea dragon, about eight inches in length from nose to tail, flitted about the porch. Three little birds perched on the railing twittered every time it went by.

A woman came out of the house carrying a deck of cards, "Shall we play *Tarot War?*" she asked him. Her body was completely covered by a chitinous integument except for her face.

"That would be lovely, Ella," he said.

"We seem to have guests," she said with a start and pointed to the two weary travelers.

"Welcome, visitors! Come up! Come up! Join us for brunchanto!" he called to them. "Some brunchanto morning, you may see a stranger, across a crowded lawn," he sang out. "You'll have to forgive me for not standing to greet you, I am still very sore from my last combat." They all shook hands and the two adventurers sat at the table. "I am the Six of Leaves. But my friends call me Roadhouse. This is Ella. Please, help yourselves," he said motioning across the table. "We also have some breakfast beer on ice over in that barrel behind you, if you like."

"Who were you fighting, if I may ask?" Alice queried.

"The Blue Tripper attacked me from out of nowhere. Craziest Chessian yet! Jumping all over the place. He shouted something about protecting Basila with his life. I can respect that. I must have wandered into the Blue Kingdom without knowing. He was quite the character, though; wearing nothing but a fustanella and a smile. He had a Florentine fighting style, even cracked my armor. Can you believe that? Powered armor! Wow. Then he bounded away."

"A maleficent game people play at," Ella said.

"Life is not a game, it is an arcade," the warrior philosopher said. "You decide *what* to play. You decide *how* to play. You decide *who you want* to play with."

"She wrapped her arms around him from her standing position behind him and said, "Well, you need to stop playing with all those ruffians and play with me more instead," then gave him a long kiss.

"You are so right, my dear."

"I don't mean to insult your hospitality," Weasel said, "but I'm a mite battle weary myself, so I'm going to catch a quick packnap before we head out."

"No problem. Make yourself comfortable. There's a hammock between the oaks on the side of the house."

"I know Jurrus, we're buddies."

Roadhouse just nodded in understanding. Dirty downed two Uhwherican eggs, hopped off the porch, then snuggled up with the snoozing night thing. Jurrus shifted slightly and half-opened one eye, "Oh, hey Weaz," then went back to sleep.

Ella took a seat next to Roadhouse.

"Would you like a sandwich?" the Six asked.
"What kind is it?" Alice enquired.
"Dark matter."

"Oh?" Alice was intrigued. "And what exactly is in a dark matter sandwich?"

He handed her one, "Look at the bread, the delicate baked lattice of the two basest ingredients required for life, flour and water. Fire, earth, and water combined to sustain the fourth element; air, the soul, the mind, the breath of life. This forms the fifth element which binds us all together, and keeps the universe expanding; aether lunch, quintessencewiches, dark energy dining."

"This is part of basket theory, correct?"

"Yes! You know what I'm talking about!"

Alice took a bite. "Mmmmmmmmm. This is the best peanut butter and jelly sandwich I've ever tasted."

"Do you know why?"

Alice pondered this question, opened the sandwich for a moment, then took another bite of the gooey goodness. "Well, the jelly is a semisolid, plasmic state of dark energy." She took another bite. "The peanut butter is the dark matter, that which makes up us, the universe, and everything else in it."

He poured her a glass of milk. "Here, you probably need a cosmic catalyst."

"Oh, yes, thank you!" She took a gulp, "Ahhh, big bango." A few more bites and another swig, "And, like you said, the bread holds it all together." She finished her sandwich and milk.

"But what makes it the best one you've ever had?"

Alice smiled, "Why, because of how it's made. With love."

"Ah, my dear, it is so wonderful to converse with someone who understands how reality works."

She added as a humorous aside, "It accelerates the expansion of the universe as part of cosmic inflation, and the expansion of the waistline as well if one is not careful."

"There is nothing wrong with being a large mammal. Hahaha! Would you like another?"

"No, thank you. But perhaps another glass of milk."

"Of course. I shall pour."

With a belly fully of stars, Alice closed her eyes and rested for a bit. She did not require much sleep. And she hated wasting time.

Alice stirred. "Do you have a water closet or similar facility that I may use?" she asked.

"This is just an old country farmhouse. The only thing we

have is an outhouse around back. None of those fancy pressurized copper pots."

"Thank you," Alice said, excusing herself, "I shall return."

She found her way to the outhouse and took off her chainsaw and rested it beside a hoary plow. She held her nose but it didn't help much while she sat in the privy and relieved herself. It was actually more of a small shed with the latrine area in one corner. Various work tools and gardening implements were stored here. She wondered if it doubled as a make-your-own fertilizer workshop. Alice heard a voice from below her, inside the pit toilet. "Mmmm. Savor the flavor. Citrusy. Thank you."

Alice yelped in surprise as she leaped off the seat and tugged up her underwear. She looked down the long drop and saw a naked man with insect wings and fly-like features sitting in the shit pile, feasting. "I'd like to eat that sunshiny pussy. Lots of juicy bacteria to slurp off that filthy thing I'll bet. Tickle tickle tongue time!"

Undeterred by his offensive comment and angered by his choice of dining area, Alice snatched a flower pot from a nearby shelf and dropped it through the opening. She heard it thud against him, probably on his upper back, as he was crouched over. It was enough to irritate him but not really hurt him. There was a buzz as he flew up the length of the shitter shaft, grabbed hold of the seat and pulled himself out.

"I can smell your twat rot from here. Delicious!" He wiggled his proboscis tongue at her. "After I suck up all that sweet sex I'm gonna literally assfuck the shit out of you. Then, after that little snack, I'm gonna give you the dipteran dick and shoot all up inside you." He tried to nab her but she was too fast for him. And since he was covered in feces, she did not want a bug hug!

He buzzed around her and blocked the only door. "My larvae will devour your corpse, which I will continue to bang and befoul, fuck and feast upon. Come to Daddy Coochie Cootie. Who's my dirty girl?"

Scanning the room, Alice saw a scattering of white crystalline pieces around a small gunny sack. Aha! She grabbed it and pulled open the top. She flung the sack at the necro fly and blinded him. He was covered in ammonium nitrate, commonly used as a high-nitrogen fertilizer, and also highly explosive.

Alice reached past him and opened the door, slamming the insectuous molester out of the way. She pulled Weasel's mechaspark lighter from her pocket, fired it up and tossed it at the outhouse fly as she bounded away.

Even with a time push she couldn't move fast enough to avoid the concussive force of the explosion as the loo blew, nothing more to skip to. It knocked her over, but at least she had avoided the burny part of the detonation. Flaming debris landed everywhere. She rolled out of range of the superheated shit rain eruption.

Weasel came running around the corner of the house. "What was that all about?"

"Pest control," Alice answered. "I owe you a lighter."

The blast had woken Jurrus as well, who helped stomp out the smattering of small fires.

"Alright, Weasel," Alice said, recovering her saw, "let's go say our goodbyes. We've got some affairs of the heart to attend to."

"Sorry about the shed," Alice said and proceeded to explain.

"Not to worry. Sounds like fly guy got what he deserved," said Roadhouse. "I've got some friends who are handy with such work; doors, windows, iron fortresses."

"Be sure to take some treats with you," Ella said. "We've got Faraday fudge, it's double slit double choclit, blackbody brownies, looking glass cake, synonym rolls, absinthe sugar plums, and some more dark matter sandwiches."

Alice chose a magic brownie and a sandwich and put them in her little basket. Weasel wrapped a couple of plums in a handkerchief and put them in his bag.

"Do you have an extra lighter or other fire starting device that we may procure? Obviously, my other one has been used up," Weasel asked.

"No sparkers," Roadhouse said. "Honey, do we have any matches in the kitchen?" he asked Ella.

"Yes. I'll get them." She returned momentarily. "Here you are, Mister Weasel."

"Thank you kindly."

"We shall take our leave," Alice said. "Thank you for your generous reception."

"Anytime," Roadhouse replied. "Come see us if you ever make it over to the Leaf Kingdom."

"Will do."

Waves and well wishes, then they were on their way.

They came to a crossroads.
"Why didn't you ask Roadhouse if he wanted to join us?" Weasel queried.
"He has a more important game to play," Alice said.
"Onward to the Heartland, then?"
"Yes."

Zuggernaut - Chapter 22

High on a shaded ridge they could make out the silhouette of an armored rider on horseback. It was the Red Knight. He made his way slowly down from his vantage point. A teen girl, dressed all in blue and of obvious Blue Chessian lineage, was trailing behind, her hands tied, a long tether attached to the saddle leading her.

"For his sake, I hope he's not looking for trouble," Alice said.

He stopped before the trekking twosome and removed his helmet. "You are, I believe, Alice."

"Yes," she said simply.

"And your companion?"

"I am Dirty Weasel," the furry fighter replied.

He bowed slightly toward each one of them, "I am Zug, the Red Knight. It is my honor to make your acquaintance. For your benevolent deed in saving the Red Sergeant from the blades of the Gambak mercenaries and befriending Dame Desultoria, the Red Kingdom is in your debt. If there is any way that I may assist you, please say."

They stood at ease knowing that he came as an ally and not an antagonist.

"You are far from home, Zug," Alice said. "You must know that you have entered the realm of the Card Kingdoms."

"Yes. Now that the Red King is dead, Blue has become more aggressive in their tactics. I was chasing the Tripper when I came across this one." He pulled the tethered girl forward. "The Blue Fox. She may look innocent but she is treacherous." She was dressed in a blue skirt and hooded jacket, with a matching tail and ears. She painted her face to give the appearance of her totem animal.

perspective

"The true savior of this wondrous land has come! She of the lilac flame. She gave me this, the mark of the Knust. Shadoobie." Blue Fox pulled up her left sleeve and showed them the religious wound on her inner forearm. "Cut in by her own hand. It means *the one who stops the heart.* I am a sliver, a disciple, a part of the whole, the big picture. Shadoobie."

"What did she carve it with, a rusty screwdriver?" Alice asked rhetorically.

"Or a chainsaw," Weasel snickered.

"Broken looking glass," Blue Fox replied. "Now she is inside me. Shadoobie." The sacred scarification had been cauterized but the slices had been deep and uneven. The burned flesh was jagged and cracked and bleeding in several places.

"Crazy like a fox, eh," Weasel said.

Blue Fox bared her teeth at him. She had filed them down to sharp points. "Would you like to find out if I am rabid? You terrible excuse for a mammal. I would devour you, vermin. Bite, bite, bite." She made a chomping motion.

Weasel mocked her by folding up the fingers on the striker automaton hand and shaking the extended index finger at her, "Now, now, young lady."

"Weasel, leave her alone," Alice said.

"Fine." He exaggeratedly rolled his eyes.

"She is fortunate that I did not catch her traveling companion, the Blue Vexer," Zug said. "All these impure Chessians. They cannot live up to their station of nobility so they turn to the faery magics. A twisted path for a twisted people."

"Ha! You'll never get Kunaozi," blurted Blue Fox.

"Now wait a minute," Alice said to Zug, "Desultoria is one of those twisted people."

"No. She has proven her self time and again on the field of battle. She was a true Red Knight before her affliction. We shall find a way to fix her."

"Fix her? She's not a broken doll," Alice said.

"Yeah! You crass, crimson, crotch cruncher!" Blue Fox yelled.

Alice turned to her, "One more word and I break your jaw."

"When the Heartstopper comes, it will be fun to kill and skin you. Turn your flesh into spice rubbed, smoked meat; tiny bite-sized cubes. Mmmm. Shadoobie."

A blurred chronopunch shut her up real quick. A line of blood trickled down from the side of her mouth. She gave Alice a big red smile, but remained silent.

"What's that shadoobie thing she keeps saying?" asked Weasel.

"It seems like a holy interjection, like amen or hallelujah. Her new messiah probably transferred something through the wound. It may be a mental tic, since organized religion tends to cause psychiatric disorders in people."

Zug interrupted, "Desultoria had a magical enchantment placed upon her. They are probably hiding a Blue Wizard who did this to her, and when I find the perpetrator, they will die."

"You don't know that," Alice said. "The violet might have been in her blood all these years, then she only changed when her body decided, when a certain age was reached, or because of her transition to knighthood. You need to support her regardless of whether she's primary, secondary, or some mixed up rainbow."

"Aye, indeed. I do, I do."

"Well, it has been an interesting encounter, to say the least. But we have an event to attend that starts in about an hour (cosmic time sense, casual conversational style). So we shall bid you farewell and I'm sure we shall meet again."

"Then I shall take my leave. Good journey." He nodded his head to each of them and turned his horse.

Blue Fox wiggled her fingers behind him and made lightning sounds, "What if *I* am the Blue Wizard?" and then gave an intentionally over-the-top maniacal laugh. "And give me back my towel, you red bastard!"

He ignored her and let the horse pull her line.

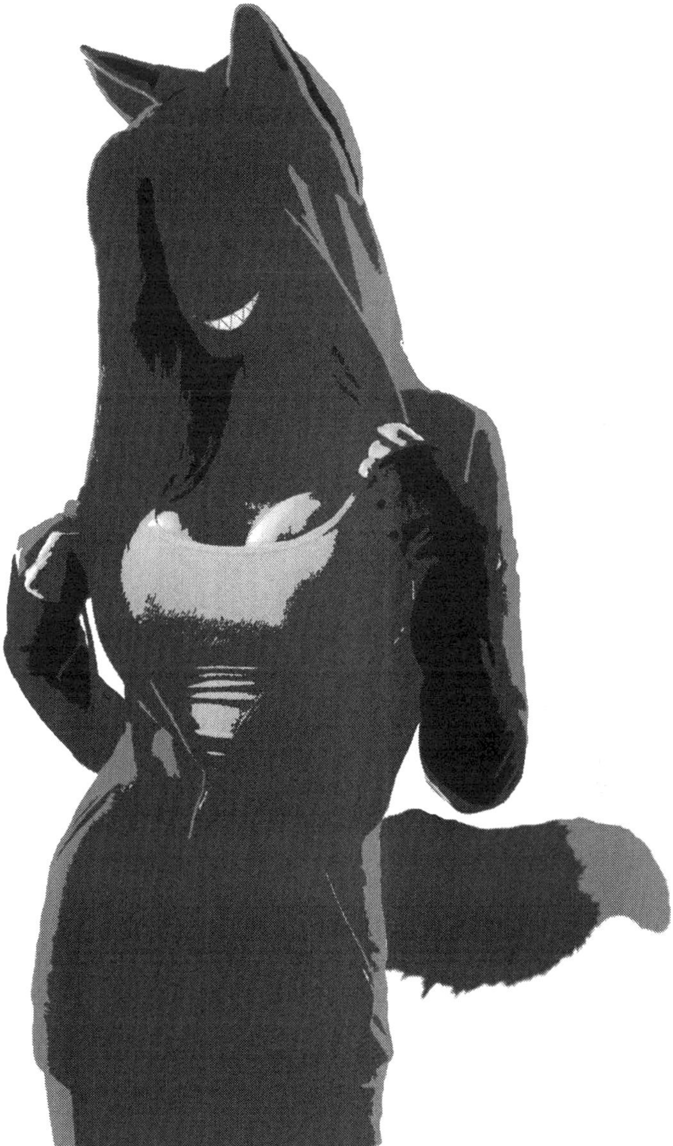

Party Smashers - Chapter 23

"I wanted to ask you about this secret breakfast I keep hearing about," Alice said.

The grounds leading to the Castle of Hearts were immaculate. Except for the white roses that some of the lower cards were painting red.

"Looks like somebody fucked up," Weasel said. "Heads will roll."

"Not today they won't. Not ever again," she replied.

Alice stopped short, then gave a discerning squint in an attempt to get a better view. She peered through a wrought iron gate that was set in the hedge wall, the makeshift shade to block the sight of passersby had been clumsily hung and was drooping. "Weasel, what does that look like to you?"

He glanced over, then did a double take, "That would appear to be the Queen of Hearts fucking a pile of dead bodies."

"Yeah, that's what I thought."

Indeed, the Queen of Hearts liked to indulge in a cold one every now and then. Quite a few and quite often, actually. Four and twenty blackbirds baked into a pie, it was not.

There is a murder of crows, a flock of seagulls, and a cackle of hyenas, but what would be the collective noun for a stack of rotting remains? A compost of corpses, perhaps?

"Let's keep going," Alice said.

"Definitely," Weasel agreed.

The queen was naked and continued rolling around on the accumulated cadavers, this pyramid of necrosex. She played coy games with her stilled partners; teasing, taunting, touching, toying, tasting.

Her petite mort was of a morbid, literal sense. She collapsed in ecstasy after her cadaverous climaxuous coitus.

The royal tub, white marble with inlaid hearts of deep red onyx, had been moved outside and a bath had been previously prepared for when her relations were done. She submerged in the warm soothing water, then stepped to the blindfolded maidservants so that they could dry her. The queen's attendant, the only one allowed eyes uncovered, aided in dressing for the afternoon's amusements.

The flush royal broke off the middle finger of one of the corpses, lifted the layers of her skirt, and inserted the stiff appendage into her vagina, "The final 'fuck you' is mine!" she announced. A piece of necrophilia memorabilia, a party favor if you will, something to keep her entertained and smiling during the dreadfully boring chitchat. She could squeeze her large thighs together just so, and cause the finger to move back and forth, just like the real thing in action.

There was a group of humanoids, tall, green and grungy, arguing with the gatekeeper, the Ten of Hearts, who was preventing them from joining the garden party. The were carrying crudely crafted, oversized croquet mallets and several had huge glass containers strapped to their backs filled with a bubbling liquid foxfire. Gamer trolls, followers of Nafjaroar. The loudest, and probably their head priest, or curmudgeon master or god moderator or whatever they call him, wore a tattered tailcoat, a floppy top hat, and a pair of goggles with half a dozen swivel-mounted magnifying loupes; a blind itinerant godgob.

Alice and Weasel marched right up to the Ten. She shoved the royal invitation in his face and kept walking.

"Um, your weapons, they must be peace-tied," the Ten sputtered.

"Try and take 'em," Weasel said.

The card guard did nothing. He did not know what to do. No one had ever disregarded noble etiquette before, even their otherworldly guests.

Alice slightly opened her satchel and pulled up the troll's holy tome so that they could see the title. "Mo Bé--Deek!" she said emphatically and patted the book, then put it back and walked in. The trolls became incensed that they were not allowed to play.

The croquet crashers entered the garden area where the party was being held. Alice scanned her surroundings.

"Looks like most of the big shots showed up," Alice said. "I wonder if they harassed the Duchess for not having her invitation?" They both chuckled.

The Duchess, Jack, and the White Rabbit were all milling about. A few dozen Heartisans were around the periphery but they were all lowballs, no studs or wild cards among them. Jack had actually cut off his broken arm and replaced it with a mechanical one. Mad science indeed.

Tuella was here and actually dressed! But some of the otherplanar guests had not been held to the same restrictions. She was wearing all white. Corset, medium tulle skirt, lace cuffs, and ankle button boots. Her hearts and spider insignia was printed on the corset. Accented, of course, by her fabulous mechanical gauntlets. A deadly beauty.

The Queen of Hearts had slipped into the party and was chatting with the Queen of Diamonds. They must be at a shaky accord. Alice half expected the Ace of Spades to burst in guns blazing at any moment.

Alice motioned discretely to Weasel while trying to remain subtle about her gesture. "We've got some new Cthuloid players in the game," she said. "The one on the left looks like what Granny Gopher was cross-stitching. Aquarii, Thomas called them."

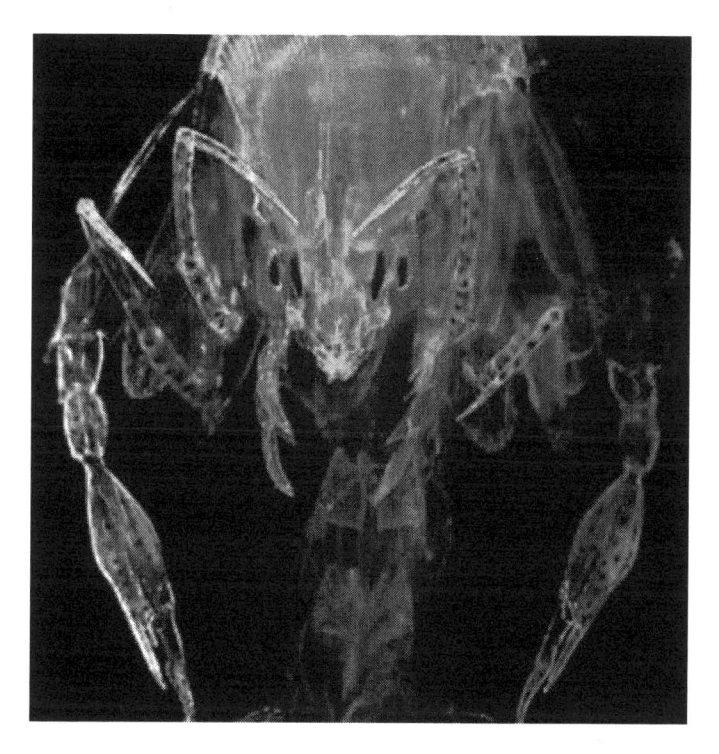

It had a female human face and torso, except she had tentacles instead of legs and another cluster of shorter, thinner tentacles growing from her head in place of hair.

She was surrounded by several creatures that hovered with no apparent means to do so. They must be harnessing one of the dark energies to maintain their lift. They had a set of claws, four piercing limbs, and a pair of helper claws probably used more for aiding in food consumption rather than for aggressive pursuits. They had an exoskeleton, and considering their mistress' suspected origin, they were probably an antipodal form of crustacean as opposed to entomous.

She was lounging in the tremendous reflecting pool. On the opposite side was a mermaid with an artificial arm. It appeared to be made of rock or coral, but she could move her arm as if it was still flesh. She was talking to a woman in casual vesture. Her hair was a dull sky blue and she almost seemed to be wrapped in wisps of clouds. Alice caught a quick glimpse of the Cheshire Cat floating lazily near her head as he synchronously faded in and out with his slowly flitting tail. She must be the Cheshire Queen.

    A young woman was sitting quietly, hands folded in her lap, on the outside edge of the pool's basin. She was not partaking in any of the conversations. She wore a medium sea foam green ball gown and a veil of woven kelp. Alice could not get a good look at her but she seemed familiar.
    Mazziel the meat angel and Andres Zachson the warp knight were sitting in a gazebo. They appeared to be very inebriated. She did not know how much help they would be, if at all.
    "Alright, let's get this party started," Alice said. "Hand me the matches and a stick of dynamite."
    "All aboard the crazy train!" Weasel said as he pulled them out.
    "Going off the rails. Distract our rabbit friend."
    "With pleasure."
    He maneuvered around in front of White, and with a toothy weaselly smile, "Hellooo, Rabbit."
    "D-d-d-dirty Weasel?!?! What are you doing here?"
    "I get invited to all the best parties."
    Alice grabbed the little lagot by the ears and pulled him close, "Do you want to know why you animals should wear pants?" She punched him in the back of the head and dazed him. Then she

rammed the stick of dynamite up his ass! This got his attention. The match was self-igniting. Alice held it and flicked the tip with her fingernail, blazing it up like a fiery flower.

Some of the denizens began to notice the commotion. Alice lit the fuse then called out to the Knave who was standing about fifteen feet away, "Hey! Jack! How's the new arm working out? CATCH!" She flung the White Rabbit at him. Jack fumbled with the loopy leaper. Then, dynamite detonation.

BOOM! No more rabbit.

"Ewww, explosive diarrhea," Weasel said laughing. The blast had knocked Jack over but not out, as Rabbit's body took the brunt of the force. Chunks of fur and gore had splattered all over Jack and Tuella.

The Two beelined for Alice. Weasel cut her off as he slid across the lawn and bashed her in the shins with the robo-arm-club, tripping her. "Do you like the taste of my metal?" he asked as he crowned her with his improvised weapon. Her head bobbed and she dropped facedown into the grass.

Alice pulled out the chainsaw and rushed Jack. He barely raised his mechanical arm in time to block the whirring killchain. Sparks flew as the blade tore apart the artificial appendage. Then Alice placed her combat boot up into his ribs, knocking the wind out of him. He folded over and fell. Jack started frantically pressing buttons on what was probably a control box like he had at the club.

"Shit. Not again," Alice said.

The other party guests chose to let the combatants fight it out rather than join.

A pounding industrial noise filled the air. The ground began shaking with a rhythmic thud. Jack's siege engine was on its way.

"Weasel! You got those other two sticks of dynamite?" Alice yelled. "Whatever's coming, its going to be big!" She gave Jack a good stomping while he was down. "You're lucky I need you alive to fix other damage you've caused or I'd have already cut you in half!"

Weasel joined her and presented the boom tubes. She reached into her pinafore pocket for the matches.

Crashing through the garden hedge came a gigantic automaton. It was over twenty feet high.

"I don't think these are going to be enough," Weasel said at the sight of the looming doomdropper.

Alice paused with a curious look on her face. "Hmmm. I've got something better." She pulled out the bottle of leftover growth elixir from Rabbit's house. She removed the stopper and finished the sweet liquid. "Titanic."

The energy drink immediately started working. But it was different this time. Alice doubled over in pain from terrible cramping. She couldn't hold onto the chainsaw.

She started growing in size and blood flowed down her legs. She felt a tearing in her vagina. Taller, taller. Her underwear bulged and rived as a full term newborn luged out of her. It dangled by the umbilical cord between giant Alice's legs. The growth potion had accelerated the gestation process. Alice was a mother!

With an exasperation of joy, the Duchess declared, "Oh! A baby! Let me help you with it!"

"Touch the child and I will kill you," Alice said. She pulled out her folding knife and severed the umbilical cord. "Weasel. Take the baby. Get out of here. Keep it safe." She lowered the child into his waiting arms.

"What about you?"

"Don't worry. I've still got. . ." The automaton slammed its tremendous metal body into Alice and they both tumbled head over heels.

Weasel fled the garden. Mazziel sent Andres Zachson to escort them and ensure their withdrawal went unchallenged.

The Deuce had come to but did not get involved. She instead summoned another card guard and sent him on an urgent errand.

Alice wrestled back and forth with the big bad bot. She was much faster but it was very heavy and difficult for her to gain leverage against. She began to pick, prod, and pull apart any panels, gears, or wires that she could get to. It began to falter and clank about as more loosened pieces fell off. She grabbed its arms, went into a time slip and pivoted the metal behemoth. She used the burst of acceleration to fling the automaton toward the castle. It smashed through the outer defensive wall then collapsed. Motionless. Kaput.

"Jack! You are ruining my party!" the Queen of Hearts bellowed! "Executioner! Where is the executioner?" she continued screaming at the top of her lungs, "Executioner! Off with his head!"

The Executioner of Hearts strode confidently down the garden path towards the queen. He wore a red tunic which bore a white heart with red X over his left breast. It covered a suit of plate armor. He carried a heavy axe, its blade stained with blood from his previous victims. "What is your bidding, my queen?"

"Rule forty-two. All persons more than a mile high are to leave the court. It does not state whether they be live or dead. Kill that giant. Then take Jack to the stocks. We shall cut off his head in the morning then have his trial in the afternoon just before tea."

"As you command. The harder they fall."

Alice was cautious to avoid the swing of his axe. Though she had the proportional advantage, the clever cleaver reeve was a veteran warrior. He could chop her down to size if she wasn't careful. She flicked his helmet with her huge fingers then laughed mockingly to see if she could intimidate or infuriate him. Alice went round and round with the X.

There was a sharp prick in Alice's calf. She started to feel dizzy. She looked back to see the Ace of Hearts holding an empty glass syringe. That was who the card guard had been sent for. Alice shrank back down to her normal size. The Ace barely made eye contact and said, "I'm sorry," in sign language, then the timid healer retreated.

Tuella moved in to enter the combat. "No!" the X shouted at her. "She is unarmed. You will back away or you will suffer at my hand. This is champion warfare between her and I. You will not dishonor me by interfering."

The Two debated whether she should test his threat but then chose to back down. "Fine. Just hurry up and kill the bitch then, if you can." She took a seat at the reflecting pool.

"You may retrieve your gardening tool, and then we shall commence where we left off."

Alice retrieved the chainsaw and they began again. Though the axe seemed unwieldy, he was strong and his motions were fluid. He would roll the handle and flip the blade to deflect her saw attacks.

She began augmenting her assault with her chronokinetic ability, accelerating her swings to a near blur. She advanced on the X and drove him back. His muscles burned from clenching the axe to keep it from being knocked away by her onslaught.

The X was hoodwinked! Alice broke from the engagement and waylayed the Queen of Hearts. She sheathed the chainsaw as she surged forth and grabbed the matriarch's bodice. She placed her hand over the royal's chest. "It's time."

Alice stopped the queen's heart.

The sovereign's eyes rolled back as she collapsed in Alice's arms. The crown fell from her head. Alice placed her gently on the lawn. The queen was dead.

The crowd was in shock.

"Always think ten moves ahead," Alice said. She had achieved what she came to do, but knew that she wouldn't be able to leave the garden as easily as she had entered.

Tuella picked up the crown. "Oops. Was I too late?" she asked with a wicked smile. She tossed the diadem to the Ace, "Here. Hold this. I guess someone has to clean up this mess of a girl."

"No. She's my responsibility," a voice interrupted. Standing beside the fallen queen was. . .Alice?

"Who are you?" asked the chainsaw champion.

"It's very simple. I am Good Alice. And you are, we'll just

call you Evil Alice. Didn't you think it strange that all the night beasts and dark denizens of this world, as well as the chthonic visitors brought here by Rabbit, so readily accepted you as one of their own? It's because you *are* one of them.

"You are the manifestation of the Cimmerian soul that was trapped inside that jar back in the rabbit hole. I cut my finger on the broken looking glass which had also fallen from the surrounding shelves. A drop of my blood must have landed in your protoplasmic clabber and mixed with you. Your darker self arose; a derisive demon, a disdainful doppelganger. You are a shadowspawn, a mockery, a thing from Plato's cave."

"How about Freethinking Alice stands up against Socially Constrained Alice? Who are you to judge me? Or what is right or wrong?"

"Isn't that the same as what you've been doing as you've rampaged across this foreign land?"

"It is not the same. I have stayed my hand where possible. I have aided and befriended many who reside here. I have slain the wicked queen who sought to conquer the surrounding lands and enslave their peoples."

"You are chaos. I am a timekeeper. Order must be kept. You are an anomaly, disruptive to the local time stream, so you must be removed--permanently."

Good Alice had retrieved the White Rabbit's shock gloves and was straining off as much of the blood and body bits as she could. They were a little tight but stretched to fit. She continued on, "Perhaps you'd like to make a vain allegation that I am the imposter and that you are the real Alice. You haven't even met your twin, Broken Alice, who rose from that same shattered looking glass. She's a real pip. Too bad you'll never meet her."

"Suck my saw."

Weapons were brought to bear and the two timefighters launched into a flurry of attacks. Good Alice avoided the cutting blade but used the electrogloves to send shocks down the length of the chainsaw. Shadow Alice stomped on her antagonist's foot with her combat boot, "Shoulda got better shoes," then delivered a solid shoulder block.

They both began quick bursts of time jumping in an attempt to get the advantage, like two Cheshire Cats fighting across multiple realities. On and on they sparred, locked in their deadly dance.

Their chronokinetic nature synchronized them to each other's moves. Freezing time, aging attacks, clock rocking, clairviolence, none of these worked on the other one. Neither could get the upper hand.

That's when the Lady of the Chain pushed her ability as hard as she could. And the superior handling of her weapon of choice made the difference. She sliced Good Alice across the right arm and chest. The wound was deep and severe. She clapped her opponent's hands together, smashing the spark mechanism in the shock gloves, rendering them useless. The progenitor backed away reeling.

"Are we done here?" asked the caliginous cutter. Good Alice just smirked.

The chainsaw was ripped away from the tenebrous tough! Then she was struck with such fury from the opposite side that it could only be a chronopunch! But the real Alice had remained unmoving in front of her. A barrage of time strikes rained down on her from every direction. She could not defend against them. She stood swaying, battered and befuddled.

Good Alice had created time doubles, mirror images of herself. She moved in for the coup de grace; a final, chronocrusher--dead on.

The shadow sister fell. "Patina, I tried..." Blackout.

And just before she hit the ground Chainsaw Alice faded away...

Epilogue

    "I thought I told you, it's not my time."

    And in all the love and chaos, the Cheshire Cat stole the Queen of Hearts' crown and was already lounging lazily upon her throne. Sneaky puss.

Did you find the hidden character?

Lovely Cthalice went to the palace
To attend the royal party
Slimy Cthalice was suffused with malice
And soon they'd all be sorry
Scary Cthalice became rather gallus
Filling her friends with fright
Crazy Cthalice seemed dreadfully callous
Because the stars were right

Ia! Ia! Cthalice fhtagn!
Ia! Ia! Have you forgotten?
Ia! Ia! Rise, doomslinger!
Ia! Ia! Fuck Kip Winger!

And YES! they had chainsaws in the Victorian Era. The chain hand saw was invented around 1783. A hand-cranked version was invented around 1830. They were primarily used for medical purposes such as cutting bone, dissection, and excision. I fact check any unsure timeframe items, words, sciences, etcetera. So don't question me, fuckers!

      Fucker - an annoying or obnoxious person; one who fucks. Origin 1590-1600.

Dress Alice for combat!

COLOR AND CUT OUT ALICE'S EQUIPMENT

"What the fuck are you doing?" the Cheshire Cat asked in a very accusatory manner. "Stop trying to read the last page to find out how it ends."

Out of space.

Out of time.

Out of control.

Made in the USA
Charleston, SC
05 February 2016